GOAT MUSIC

GOAT MUSIC

Will Buckingham

ROMAN *Books*
www.roman-books.co.uk

ISBN 978-93-83868-06-3

Typeset in Adobe Garamond Pro

First published in 2015

1 3 5 7 9 8 6 4 2

British Library Cataloguing in Publication Data
A catalogue record for this book is available from the British Library.

Publisher: Suman Chakraborty

ROMAN Books
26 York Street, London W1U 6PZ, United Kingdom
Unit 49, Park Plaza, South Block, Ground Floor, 71 Park Street, Kolkata 700016, WB, India
2nd Floor, 38/3 Andul Road, Howrah 711109, WB, India
www.roman-books.co.uk | www.romanbooks.co.in

Printed and bound in India by
Repro India Ltd

All his body was covered with hair and bristles, and yet—good heavens! he is said to have striven for mastery with Apollo. 'Twas hideousness contending with beauty, a rude boor against a sage, a beast against a god . . .

—Apuleius

Goat Music, a Satyr Play
Dramatis Personae

Marsyas	A Phrygian satyr
Kybele	Mother-goddess of Phrygia
Dionysos	God of wine, half brother of Apollo
Apollo	God of music, medicine and mice
Hermes	Messenger god, brother to Apollo
Midas	King of Phrygia and son of Kybele
Orpheus	Musician, lover and poet
Tmolos	Mountain god of Phrygia
Athene	Goddess of war
Kharon	A ferryman
Zeus	Ruler of the Olympians

Along with assorted Mortals, Gods, Goats, Satyroi, Seilenoi, &c.

PART I
SATYR

1

It was a time and it was no time, for time had not yet learned that it was a river. And in this time that was no time, there was a mountain somewhere in Phrygia, its sides thick with trees and tangled shrubs. A clear stream tumbled into the valley below, and not far from the stream was a creature, making its way down a rugged path. It moved with the speed and light delicacy of a goat, yet it went on two feet instead of four.

It was early spring. Lizards warmed themselves on the rocks in the sun. Insects filled the air with their thrum and chirr, blue and green dragonflies darted and hovered between the sighing reeds. High above, a bird of prey mewled for its mate. Further off, wild animals roamed the hillsides: lions, leopards, bears and wolves, caracals, jackals and creatures long forgotten, or that today we know only by their names: seilenoi, kentauroi and satyroi.

The creature making its way down the mountain was a satyr. Its name—or *his* name, for he was most distinctly male—was Marsyas. He was a favourite of the corn goddess, Kybele, and half brother or stepbrother—nobody was very sure which—of the divine singer Orpheus. The satyr scampered down the precipitous path with nimble-footed eagerness, his cock alert as a hound before the hunt.

Although his upper half was almost human, below he was mostly goat except, where one might have expected to find cloven hooves, there were instead long, flexible toes. His legs were shagged with brown hair, his little buttocks covered in a reddish fur. Between his legs, his cock—somewhat long, with an elegant double curve—was half risen; and behind him was a short and brushy tail that he could swish to keep away the flies.

A ribbon of auburn fur ran up his pink belly, the same fur that covered his back and chest. His arms were those of a human being, the fingers a little longer than usual; and his face was more that of a bearded man in life's prime than of a goat, except his eyes, overhung with bushy brows, had oblong yellow pupils. His velvety ears glowed in the sunlight, the veins dark channels, rivers of blood running through the delta of his illuminated flesh. Two small goat horns poked through his rough and wiry hair.

The satyr had a tune in his head, a melody of such exquisite beauty that it was all he could do not to open his mouth and sing. The music made him think of the pleasures of love and made his cock twitch. But he did not sing, for he had made a binding oath before the goddess Kybele. The memory of this oath brought him a sharp stab of unhappiness. Then the tune passed out of his head and the sadness dissipated. Marsyas found it was hard to keep anything in his head for long. He sniffed the air again and scampered onwards to where the path bordered a small copse of oak and beech.

On his left, the leaves were fresh with the hopeful greens

of springtime, darkening to black as the foliage thickened. To the other side of the path, the slope was steep and precipitous. Marsyas was not afraid of heights: on rocks and precipices, he moved with the easy freedom of a goat.

As he was passing the copse, he scented something. The smell was unfamiliar. He hesitated.

A voice came from out of the foliage. It was spoken rather than sung, but strangely melodious. 'Oooohhhaaaa!' it said.

Marsyas hopped backwards onto a rock by the precipice. He stared into the darkness of the copse.

'Oooohhhaaaa!' said the voice.

'Hello,' Marsyas bleated.

'Oooohhhaaaa!'

There was a rustling in the leaves. From out of the darkness emerged the figure of a youth. He was naked, his limbs brown and well formed, almost feminine. His chest was virtually hairless, but on his chin there was a few days' growth of beard. He wore an ivy crown upon his head, and by his side there bulged a goatskin flask. Marsyas felt a pang of unease at the sight of the skin. He sniffed the air again. He could smell leaf mould and decay.

The youth stepped unsteadily onto the path. When his eyes fell upon Marsyas, they opened wide. They were the most beautiful eyes Marsyas had ever seen, dark and deep and filled with exquisite suffering. The youth's red lips twitched upwards into a smile.

Marsyas was intrigued. He leaned forwards. 'Who are you?' he asked. 'I've not seen you before.'

'I am godspawn,' the youth said. His words were slurred and the smell of decay was on his breath.

'You're what?' asked Marsyas.

'I am godspawn,' the youth repeated. 'I am goatspawn and I am manspawn.' The muffled syllables were hard to catch, and there was something about the youth that seemed a little dangerous. But there was also something pathetic, something absurd. Marsyas suppressed a snicker. The youth took a pace forward. Marsyas hopped from the rock to take a closer look.

The youth was a couple of heads taller than Marsyas, so that the satyr came only up to his chest. The youth looked down into Marsyas's oblong eyes, and then he leaned in to kiss him, once, upon the lips. 'You must be Marsyas,' the youth said softly. He rested his forehead on Marsyas's own. 'I have heard about you. You are Kybele's boy.'

The satyr looked into those deep, sad eyes. They made him excited and uneasy, both at the same time.

'I am your brother,' the youth whispered. 'Like you, I was once a goat fed on honey . . .' Then his eyes lost their focus, he lifted his head, he swayed a little, and he fell down on all fours.

Like a beast, the youth vomited.

Marsyas's nostrils flared at the acrid stench. The youth retched again. Then he looked up at the satyr with a sly smile. He sat back on his haunches, took the skin from his side, and held it out. 'I bring you wine,' he slurred. 'It is a gift that will bring you joy and despair in equal measure.'

Marsyas took the goatskin and put it to his lips. He had to suppress the impulse to gag. He filled his mouth and he swallowed.

The taste of the wine was good.

2

Together they drank until the wineskin ran dry. Then they slept in each other's arms.

Marsyas woke the following morning with a terrible sickness in his head. His tongue was rough in his mouth, but his mind had a strange, chill clarity. Somewhere in his belly, despite the undertow of lingering sickness, he had a hunger to drink more.

He rolled onto his side and propped himself up. He lifted the wineskin they had abandoned the night before and put it to his lips, but there were no more than a few drops remaining. Marsyas let his head sink back onto the grass where the youth was snoring softly. He reached down to put his hand on the youth's belly, then moved it down towards his cock, coiled and brown like a sleeping centipede. He touched it gently and the youth stirred. Marsyas, taking fright, moved his hand away.

'I am godspawn . . .' the youth said.

'Yes, yes,' said Marsyas. 'You've told me that already.' He leaned over the youth and looked at him closely.

'Goatspawn . . .' the youth said. 'Manspawn . . .'

Then the youth began to sob and Marsyas, moved to ungoatly compassion, snuggled into him and licked his neck. 'What's wrong, beautiful boy?' he murmured. 'What's wrong?'

And the youth said, 'Take me to Kybele.'

Marsyas took the youth by the hand and eased him to his feet. The youth reached down and took hold of the empty wineskin. 'We need more wine,' he said. 'Always more wine.'

Marsyas let the youth put an arm around his furry shoulders. 'Tell me your name,' the satyr said softly. 'What should I call you?'

The youth hesitated. 'I have many names,' he said. 'Some call me Pseudanor, the False One. Others Erikryptos, the Completely Hidden, or Agrios, the Wild One, or Eleutherios, the One Who Liberates, or Melanaigis, Bearer of the Black Goatskin. Or Aegobolus.'

'Aegobolus?' Marsyas asked.

'The Killer of Goats,' the youth said. Then he laughed in a way that Marsyas found frightening.

Marsyas wriggled free from him. 'Killer of Goats?' he asked, eyes wide.

'But Friend of Satyrs,' the youth said.

Marsyas thought for a moment. He looked mistrustful. 'So what should *I* call you?' he asked. 'I can't remember all those names.'

'Call me Dionysos,' the youth said. 'God of Mount Nysa.'

Marsyas peered a little closer. 'You don't *look* like a god. You've got pimples, for a start.'

Dionysos raised a hand to the side of his face. There were indeed a few pimples forming beneath the thin growth of beard. They would need bursting later. 'I may or may not be a god,' he said, 'but I am *definitely* mad and *definitely* drunk. Please, Marsyas. Take me to Kybele. She will cure me. I will see that you are rewarded.'

The satyr took the hand of the god. 'Then come,' he said.

3

As the sun started to sink across the hills, Kybele rose from her rest. She was weary and ill at ease. She sat for a moment, propped on back-turned hands. Then she stretched and rolled her massive shoulders, easing the tightness out of her spine. She reached up to fix a skein of loose, blonde hair, twisting and braiding it skilfully, and as her fingers did their quick work, she glanced over at her lions. They were still asleep, their flanks shuddering in the afternoon sun.

Kybele had spent the morning alone, with only the lions for company. She had come up into the mountains to get some peace. Here she could breathe the clear air and think of old times, when men were few and timid, when the world was young. Now, when she looked beyond the mountains, she saw men spreading everywhere like termites. She thought how industrious and stupid they were. They spent their days heaving the earth to and fro, building walls, towers and cities, putting to flight the lions, leopards, caracals, porcupines and jackals. They planted crops and fought wars. They built roads and smelted bronze out of copper from the island of Kupros and tin from who knows where.

Kybele spat, just once, on the ground. She watched the blob of sputum as it sank into the dry soil. Then she hitched up her robes and stood. Her skin was the brown of ripened wheat, her white shift stained with dust and sweat. A cord fastened the robe beneath the globes of her breasts. She flexed her toes in the soft soil and tightened the cord. Then she clucked her tongue at the lions. The big cats stretched and yawned.

'Come,' she said. 'We have work to do.'

The lions got to their feet and trotted to her side. Together, the three of them set off for the valleys of Phrygia. It was the season of planting, and life was busy.

As Kybele made her way down the mountain path, she passed the old pine tree that stood at the foot of the track. There she remembered the boy Attis. The image was sharp as knapped flint. It made her wince. She had loved Attis, but he had betrayed her in the arms of a river-god's daughter. She had punished him for that, struck him with madness. She could still picture him, standing with feet apart, laughing up at the sky, a jagged knife in his left hand, and in his right the fruit of the manhood that he had cut from his own body. Between his legs flowered a red-black hole. When she turned him into a pine tree, she was not sure whether it was to end his misery or her own. But if Attis had been punished, her own punishment was greater. When there is no forgetting, memory becomes clearer, more crystalline and perfect with every revisiting. *Attis*, she thought, reaching out to touch the trunk of the tree. *Attis, my boy. How you bled. How you cut yourself.*

But then she was distracted by a sound a little way off. It was Marsyas, heading towards the mountain path, hand in hand with a dark youth, chattering and prattling as he came. 'Marsyas,' she said. 'Who have you brought?'

Marsyas waved. 'A friend,' he said. 'He's mad. His mind is completely broken.'

Kybele beckoned them over. She was twice the height of the little satyr. She reached down to embrace him. Then she put her hand to Dionysos's cheek and looked into his eyes, seeing the madness that was there. The god looked back up at her, his eyes dark.

I will cure him, she thought. *I will make him whole again.* The symmetry was pleasing to her. She had driven the beautiful Attis insane; but now she would take this beautiful youth, already mad, and she would heal him.

Kybele sat herself down on a rock. 'Come, my little goatling,' she said, unlacing her tunic. 'Come, and bring your friend with you.'

The satyr hopped into the goddess's lap. Her flesh was cool and soft. She smelled as fresh as mountain grass. Kybele lifted out a breast from her robe and Marsyas started to suckle. The beautiful Dionysos stood, wavering and drooling. Kybele smiled at him and beckoned him towards her, tugging at her tunic to free her other breast.

4

Dionysos nestled close to Kybele, and the satyr and the god suckled side by side, like two goat-kids. When they had done, Kybele brushed the curls back from Dionysos's forehead. 'Tell me your name,' she said.

'He's called Dionysos,' said Marsyas, wiping the milk from his mouth with his furry forearm. 'And lots of other things besides, if I could remember them.'

'The little god from Nysa,' Kybele smiled. 'So *that* is who you are. Well, Dionysos, welcome. Stay with us in Phrygia a while. I will make you well.'

Dionysos, woozy with milk, said nothing. Kybele lifted him from her lap and laid him down on the grass. In a moment he was asleep.

Spring turned to summer and the goddess nurtured Dionysus. She laid her cool hand upon his brow, gave him milk to drink, coddled like the child he still was. He recovered slowly, but something about him remained strange and wayward. The mind is like a pot that, once broken, can never be fully restored. Even the most patient of repairs will leave behind spiderwebs of cracks and fractures, points of weakness where, if the pot struck again, it is liable once more to shatter. The god's madness eased, but Dionysos was unruly. He pissed in the clear mountain streams where Kybele told him not to piss. He pulled the tails of the lions when they were sleeping. One moment he was discourteous and sullen, the next he was wheedling and charming. Some days he slept and moped, on others he could be found frenziedly leaping across the mountainsides, babbling in a language only he himself could understand.

Because the god was restless and in need of a task to occupy him, Kybele put him to work as the driver of her lion chariot. It delighted him to snap the reins, and to have the lions gallop ahead of him as the chariot careered down the mountainside. As for Marsyas, he was pleased to have Dionysos around, delighted to have found such a pretty thing to play with.

Some time in early summer, Dionysos went missing. Marsyas woke in the late afternoon to find him gone. A tear formed in his oblong eye and he ran bleating to the goddess. Kybele sighed and scratched the satyr behind the ears to soothe him. 'Do not worry, Marsyas, he cannot be far. We will go and search for him.'

They departed on foot, leaving the lions to their sleeping. It was already night when they found him, down in the valley. The moon was already high, and from the middle of a small Phrygian village came the sound of great commotion. There was a clattering of drums and a clashing of korybantes' shields. Men, women, children, their voices all intermingled, hooted and shrieked. Dogs barked. Shepherds tootled on reed pipes that they had whittled whilst tending their sheep. In the centre of the village there blazed a fragrant pyre built of spitting pine logs. Behind the pyre, raised up on a makeshift platform of boulders, and twined about with ivy, was Dionysos. He held a bunch of grapes in his right hand and a goblet in his left. In front of him were ten large jars. A rabble of half naked villagers danced hand-in-hand with scampering satyroi and leering seilenoi. They tripped and fell, lay prone on the ground, then struggled to their feet again, and rejoined the dance. As they passed the amphorae of dark wine, they dipped in their hands and lifted their cupped palms to their mouths to drink. From beyond the circle of light cast by the fire came the sound of many couplings: groans and mutterings of ecstasy and of joy.

Marsyas was entranced. He scampered from Kybele's side to join the fray, plunging his furry arms into the wine jars and scooping out great palmfuls of wine. The god Dionysos looked down from his platform and saw his little friend drinking deeply, and the god laughed. The satyr linked arms with other revellers and danced. His cock waved cheerfully in the firelight. The village girls giggled. The crude music of shepherds and korybantes inflamed his heart.

It was then, intoxicated by wine and by the dance, that Marsyas forgot his promise.

He opened his mouth wide, tipped back his head, closed his eyes, and started to sing.

'*Maaaeee-he-he . . .*'

All at once, there was the sound of shrieking. A peasant girl who had been dancing next to Marsyas fell to the floor, screaming. Something dark came from her ears. In the firelight it looked like thick wine, except it was salt rather than sweet.

'*Maaaeee-he-he . . .*' the satyr sang.

Another shriek. Two more peasants fell to their knees, hot fountains of dark blood bursting from their ears. Satyroi and seilenoi ran for cover. The korybantes dropped their drums and swords and shields, and they scarpered. The musicians let fall their pipes and ran, screaming, away from the circle of light thrown by the fire. Villagers scrabbled at the soil, filling their ears with fistfuls of earth to blot out the sound.

Oblivious, on fire with the bliss of artistic creation, Marsyas continued to bleat and sing.

'*Maaaeee-he-he . . . Maaaeee-he-he . . . Maaaeee-he-he . . .*'

Dionysos leapt down from his platform. The sinews of his body taut with anger, he took the satyr by his left horn, and dragged him to the wine-vats. He thrust the satyr's head into the dark liquid.

'Maaaeee-he-he . . .
'Maaaeee-he-he . . .
'Maaaeee-he-he . . .
'Bloop . . . Bloop . . .
'Blop . . .'

The song turned to a bubbling and a spluttering. Dionysos held the Marsyas's head under until the satyr's legs began to kick and quiver. Then he pulled him out and shoved him to the ground. 'You little piece of goat shit,' the god snarled. 'If you ever do that again I will drown you for good.'

And Marsyas, because he was a sensitive and artistic soul, let out a plaintive bleat and broke down in tears.

It was then that Kybele spoke, from somewhere in the darkness where the light of the fire didn't reach. 'Marsyas, Dionysos, come with me.'

The goddess stepped into the light of the fire. She was pale and terrible, and she held out her arms. It was more a command than an invitation. Marsyas—bewildered, drunk and terrified—ran towards her and leapt into her embrace. She let the wine-soaked bundle huddle into her right breast, and put out her left hand for Dionysos. The god, his rage dissipating, slunk over and put his hand in hers.

'Let us go,' Kybele said.

Together, the three of them made their way back up towards the mountain, Dionysos clasping the hand of the goddess and Marsyas, wine-soaked and stinking, shivering in the crook of her other arm.

Before they had gone far, dawn came up over the mountains. Down in the valley, three peasants, having washed the blood from their ears, gazed upon a world grown silent.

5

By the time they reached the mountain grove where the lions were sleeping, Marsyas was snoring. Dionysos was sulking. The lions stirred. The he-lion lazily opened one eye then closed it again. Kybele placed the satyr down on the ground, taking care not to wake him. Dionysos sat next to the goddess and plucked at the grass like a spoiled child.

Kybele watched the dawn light spreading over the hills. Then she sighed and called for the lions. The beasts stretched and got to their feet. They trotted towards her, stopping on the way to sniff at Marsyas. The satyr woke immediately, letting out a small yelp of alarm—he had never trusted the lions—and scampered off to take sanctuary behind a nearby boulder. He trembled as he peered over the boulder, watching the lions settle down by Kybele's feet. The goddess ran her fingers idly through the he-lion's mane.

'Now Marsyas,' the goddess said, 'why are you hiding? Have my lions ever harmed you? Come, there is no need to fear.'

Marsyas whimpered but did not move. Dionysos smirked.

A hint of sharpness entered Kybele's voice. 'Marsyas! They have no taste for goat flesh.'

The satyr crept from behind the boulder and tiptoed over. He crouched on his haunches, and plucked a blade of grass, which he put it in his mouth to chew. Kybele looked at him sternly. 'Marsyas,' she said, 'you stink of wine. Go and wash in the stream. When you are done, come back here.'

Marsyas's eyebrows twitched angrily. He resented being given orders. But then he got to his feet and headed down the hill. Dionysos and Kybele could hear him muttering and splashing, not far off. When he returned, his fur was gleaming and wet.

Kybele patted her lap. The satyr stepped past the lions and hopped up. He gazed at the face of the goddess, trying to read her mood.

Kybele sighed. 'Marsyas,' she said softly, 'you *promised* me you would not sing.'

'I'm sorry, Kybele.'

'I should punish you.'

'But Kybele . . .' the satyr protested, 'I was *born* singing.'

The goddess tweaked his ear. 'Oh, my little goatling,' she said sadly, 'what *are* we going to do with you?'

Marsyas was more or less an orphan, although Kybele treated him with all the indulgence of a mother. Nobody was certain who the satyr's father was—some said Hyagnis, others Olympos, still others Oiagros—but whoever he was, he had never seen fit to make himself known. As for his actual mother, the day on which Marsyas was born had also been the day of her death.

Marsyas's mother had given birth alone, without friend, or kin or midwife by her side. She groaned and writhed on the soft grass of a secluded mountain grove, and offered up prayers to the goddess Eileithyia. The birth went as well as any birth can. The child struggled free from the cooking pot of his mother's womb and popped his head out into the world. Then he flopped onto the grass, opened his lips, and started to sing.

'*Maaaeee-he-he . . . Maaaeee-he-he . . . Maaaeee-he-he . . . Maaaeee-he-he . . .*'

It was his first goat-song, his first *tragōidia*. At the sound of his voice, his mother's body convulsed. She threw back her head and let out a terrible cry. Blood flowed from her ears.

Her heart stopped beating.

The infant Marsyas sensed that something was wrong. 'Mum!' he bleated. 'Mum! *Mum!*' His mother did not reply.

The newly hatched goatling chewed through the umbilical cord and scampered away.

That evening, an old seilenos found him shivering on the hillside. It was a cold night, and the seilenos took pity on him. He gave Marsyas food and drink, then he led him to the goddess Kybele, who accepted him into her care, on the condition that he made a solemn vow never to sing again—neither in the hearing of mortals, nor of immortals, nor in solitude, nor to the winds and the reeds and the trees.

The vow pained him. Often, as the sunlight fell upon the mountainside, his spirit fluttered in his breast, and his heart swelled with the desire to burst into joyful song. But he had to suppress the impulse. And when his satyr brothers sang and danced, he had to sit out and watch, unable to join the game. All he had ever wanted, from the moment of his birth, was to be a musician, to sing for an audience and to have them clap and cheer and stamp their feet. But his vow prevented him. Until the night before, that is. Wine is a great destroyer of vows.

'Marsyas,' Kybele said, scratching his ears. 'You are such a bad little satyr.'

'But Kybele, I couldn't *stop* myself,' Marsyas protested.

'That is what worries me,' Kybele said. 'Once broken, a vow is easily broken a second time. We cannot have you running around singing, Marsyas. It would be a disaster.'

Marsyas started to sob. His body shook, and his tears fell into the goddess's lap. 'Shhh . . .' she whispered. 'Shhh . . .'

Then Dionysos, whose moods were fickle and whose sulkiness seemed to have left him, looked up. 'I have an idea,' he said.

The goddess turned to him. 'An idea?' she asked.

'I have heard rumours,' Dionysos said. 'They may be to our advantage.'

6

The tale that Dionysos told Kybele and Marsyas was a strange one. How he had come by it was anybody's guess—even Dionysus himself was not entirely clear on its provenance. It concerned the goddess of war and belligerence, Athene, who had long been in dispute with Here and Aphrodite about which of the three was more beautiful. One day, the rumour went, the goddess was walking the earth stirring up wars and trouble when she sat down to rest by the side of a stream. Idly, she plucked a pair of reeds. She whittled and pierced them with her spear until she had fashioned an instrument, a double pipe. When she put the instrument to her lips and blew, she discovered the pipes made the sweetest music. She called the instrument an *aulos*.

Marsyas wriggled on Kybele's lap and interrupted Dionysos's story. 'Athene could blow my pipe any time,' he said.

Kybele gave his ear a sharp tweak. 'You will get in trouble for saying that kind of thing,' she warned. 'Those goddesses are not kind.' Then she turned to the god. 'Go on, Dionysos. Go on with your tale.'

Dionysos continued with the story. He told them how

Athene returned with the pipes to Olympos, certain that by adding the loveliness of this sweet music to the beauty of her form, she would be proclaimed the most beautiful.

That evening, when the gods were gathered in the feasting hall to eat and drink, she pulled out the aulos and played. She expected adulation, wonderment, praise. But instead, she heard Zeus's loud, mocking laugh. '*Ha! Ha! Ha!*'

The other gods joined in: Aphrodite tittered girlishly, Apollo brayed, Here cackled, Hermes sniggered, and Hephaistos bellowed in mirth. Athene was bewildered. She fled, aulos in hand, back to the earth. The goddess took refuge by the side of a clear mountain pool where, to soothe her ruffled pride, she picked up her pipes and played.

As she played, she looked into the clear stream. It was then that she understood the reason for the gods' laughter. Gazing up at her from the water was a hideous creature with bulging eyes and blue, swollen cheeks. Its lips were puckered around a pipe. And Athene knew that the monster was herself.

Marsyas's eyes widened. 'What happened next?' he asked.

'Then,' said Dionysos, 'she cast the flute aside.'

Kybele looked at Dionysos. He was cooking something up, but she was not sure what. 'Dionysos,' she said, 'why do you tell us this story?'

Dionysos gave a sly grin. 'Everybody knows that Marsyas is a great artist,' he said.

Marsyas felt an upsurge of pride. Kybele gave Dionysos a warning look. The satyr did not need any encouragement after the disaster of the night before. 'The only problem is,' the god continued, 'that the satyr's music is too powerful for mortal ears. Like wine given to children, it is too potent.'

'And so?' Kybele asked.

'And so, just as a child cannot drink wine undiluted, and the power of wine must be mediated by the admixture of water, so too does Marsyas's talent need the meditating power of a second thing. Only then will the music be fit for the ears of gods and mortals.'

Kybele smiled. Dionysos was a clever god. 'You are wise, Dionysos,' she said. 'Tell us more.'

The satyr, slow to catch on, frowned.

'Marsyas,' the god said, 'what I am saying is this: your voice, like wine, is too intoxicating. But perhaps this aulos will mediate between the greatness of your art, and the ears of gods and men.'

Marsyas's frown deepened.

'Let me put it plainly,' said Dionysos. 'Go and find Athene's pipes. Then, whenever you are taken by a desire to sing, instead you can play.'

A grin started to form on Marsyas's face. 'And where do I find the pipes?' he asked.

'I am told that Athene abandoned them in a field in Arkadia where they were found by an old shepherd. Having no use for them himself, he gave them to a band of satyroi. The aulos is still in their keeping. Go to Arkadia, Marsyas. Find the pipes. The aulos will be as water to the wine of your genius, and you can be a musician as you have always wished.'

Kybele was delighted by the elegance of Dionysos's suggestion. But a troubled look came over Marsyas's face. He frowned and looked down at his toes. The god and the goddess exchanged glances. 'What is worrying you, Marsyas?' Kybele asked.

'I'd like to play this aulos,' the satyr said, 'but I'm afraid.'

'Afraid of what?' the goddess asked.

'I'm afraid that if I play, the pipes will destroy my beauty, as they destroyed the beauty of Athene.'

Then both Dionysos and Kybele laughed. And—although he did not understand the reason for their laughter—so as not to feel left out, Marsyas joined in, letting out little panting bleats.

The goddess smiled down at the giggling satyr. Then she became serious. 'Dionysos's counsel is good,' she said. 'But promise me one thing. Once you have found the pipes, do not play them until you are back here in Phrygia. Only here are you under my protection.'

'All right,' said Marsyas.

'Do you swear?'

Marsyas hopped off Kybele's lap. Then, as solemnly as he was able, he took his cock in his hand and swore the satyr oath. 'I swear by my whopper,' he said.

The goddess reached down and kissed him on the forehead, by way of a blessing.

Excited by the thought of the journey ahead, Marsyas did a little dance. As he danced, he pulled terrible faces, like a goddess made ugly by puffing and blowing. Dionysos, delighted by this display of dancing and face-pulling, joined in. Their quarrels forgotten, the two of them danced a jig together. Marsyas bleated with joy and Dionysos whooped and shrieked in reply.

Kybele watched them both for a while. Then she got to her feet, gave a soft hiss to call her lions and, without saying goodbye, she walked away.

PART II

AULOS

7

The following morning, when Marsyas came to say goodbye to Kybele, he was surprised to find her with Dionysos, and the two of them discussing journeys and travels. 'Dionysos,' Marsyas said, 'are you coming to Arkadia with me?'

'No,' the god smiled. 'I have other business. I am going to India.'

'India?' Marsyas had not heard the name before.

'It is land of many strange gods,' said Dionysos. 'I am taking them the gift of wine.'

'Oh,' said Marsyas. He had been hoping for a companion on the road. At the thought that he might have to part from Dionysos, tears started to bead in the corners of his eyes.

Dionysos crouched down so that he was face-to-face with the satyr. 'Marsyas, I will not forget you. I will not forget how you saved me from my madness,' he said.

'Do you promise, Dionysos?'

'I promise,' the god said. He embraced the satyr, and then the goddess Kybele. 'Marsyas,' he said, 'we will meet again. And when we do, things will not be as they are now'.

And with this strange farewell, the god Dionysos slipped away out of sight among the trees.

Later that morning, Marsyas said goodbye to Kybele and headed west. At first he was sorrowful and lonely, but before he had gone too long, he forgot his sadness. He was too excited by new scents, new horizons, new encounters. He travelled through Lydia towards the coast, where he turned south and joined the course of the river Maiandros. He made his way at an easy pace, stopping off as the whim dictated, sharing food with shepherds and his satyr brothers, sleeping wherever and with whomever he happened to find himself.

By the time he reached the port of Miletos, summer was over and autumn had just begun. It was late afternoon when he saw the city walls, looming on the horizon like great and gloomy cliffs. Marsyas felt a darkening of his spirit. He passed through the gates and he was struck by the stench and uproar of the city. A hundred languages intermingled. Phrygians jostled with Lydians, Greeks with Phoenicians. And Marsyas had the dark premonition that some day all men would live like this, in noise and squalor, far from the streams, the soft green hillsides, and the cool, wooded groves.

He made his way down to the docks, following the sharp tang of salt upon the air. As he scurried through the narrow streets, he was assailed by a barrage of hisses, by gobbets of spittle and rains of curses. The people of Miletos had no liking for satyrs, even though most of them had never even set eyes on one. Some even claimed that seilenoi and kentauroi and satyroi did not exist, and so they found it an affront to the equipoise of their minds to see Marsyas scampering through the streets.

Down by the harbour were rows of ships: pentekonters,

Phoenician biremes, swift messenger ships and broad merchant vessels. People were loading and unloading cargo, carrying crates and jars of who knows what. Burly oarsmen rested against the harbour wall, trading obscenities.

Marsyas started to ask around. 'Is anybody going to Lakedaimonia?' he asked. 'Can I have a lift?'

In reply, he received only blows and imprecations.

Nobody wishes to have a satyr in a boat. A satyr in a boat is an inauspicious thing, a temptation to the Moirai, goddesses of misfortune. Some might have overlooked the horns that grew upon his head, the goatish tail that graced his arse, and his legs shagged with long fur, if only he had something to trade. To have nothing that could be exchanged: this was the worst of crimes in a city such as Miletos.

Marsyas found a quiet spot near the harbour wall, beside a heap of old, tangled fishing nets. He made himself as inconspicuous as a satyr in a city can, and he watched the commerce of the docks. Some way off, a flurry of gulls squabbled over a pile of stinking fish guts. For the first time in his life, Marsyas felt the strange aloneness that is the gift of the *polis*, the aching solitude that comes from passing in the street multitudes who will always remain strangers.

Then Marsyas caught sight of a man who seemed, by his bearing and the purple of his robe, to be a person of some consequence. He was standing on the deck of a small trading bireme, looking out to sea, hugging his robe towards his body to keep away the chill breeze coming off the sea. The way that the man gazed towards the horizon, his eyes half-narrowed, suggested a certain vanity.

This, Marsyas thought, is the man who will guarantee my passage.

Marsyas crept down to harbour-side. Very quietly, so that the merchant did not turn round, he clambered onto the vessel and hid himself amongst a pile of wooden crates. Peering from the darkness, he could see the merchant sniff the air, as if he had caught a scent that was displeasing to him. But then the merchant shrugged and fixed his eyes once again on the horizon. Beneath him, Marsyas felt the lift and fall of the boat on the swell of the sea.

The sun set. The lights of distant boats and torches glimmered in the night, reflected on the surface of the waves. The merchant turned his eyes away from the horizon and sighed. Judging that this was the right moment, Marsyas crept out of his hiding place and let out a bleat. '*Maaaeee-he-he!*' he said. 'Good evening.'

The merchant turned. His eyes widened with terror and he clasped his robe around his body more tightly. A satyr? In Miletos? On his own boat? Was it possible?

Then the merchant regained his composure. He reached into his robe and pulled out a short staff, the length of a man's forearm. He lifted it against the dark sky. 'Get off my boat, goat,' he said.

Marsyas scrambled to his feet and took a few steps back. He gave a courteous bow. 'I am not here to harm you,' he said. 'My name's Marsyas, and I'm going to Arkadia. And you, my splendid purple-clad friend, are going to take me.'

8

The merchant raised an eyebrow. For a few moments he didn't say anything at all. Then he stepped towards Marsyas, his beard quivering. 'I don't know how you got here, goat,' he said, 'but I don't have the time for this. Now shoo, unless you want a taste of the ocean.'

Marsyas cocked his head to one side and smiled. His white teeth gleamed in the moonlight. 'You are not going to Lakedaimonia, are you?' he asked. 'Or perhaps to Argos? Either would do.'

The merchant pointed the end of his staff at Marsyas. 'What's it to you where I'm going, goat boy?' he said. 'I've got oil and wine and dyes to trade. Good quality stuff. If I wanted my boat to stink of goat, I'd have become a cheese merchant.'

Marsyas gave another, deeper, bow. 'But you do *really* want to take me, don't you? I know you do.'

The merchant laughed. There was something amusing about the cringing, genuflecting satyr. He lowered his staff. 'Why would I want a satyr on my boat?' he asked.

'I can provide tail winds to speed your journey,' said Marsyas.

Then he turned his back, looked over his shoulder, and let out a resounding fart.

Pap-pap-pap-pap-pax.

For several days, Marsyas had been marinating a ripe stew in his bowels; and now that the gases were released, they were thick and pungent. The merchant raised a hand to cover his mouth and nose. He lifted his staff in the air and brought it whistling down on Marsyas's impertinent rear end. The satyr, having anticipated just such a move, scuttled out of the way just in time. The staff met with the wooden boards of the deck. A jolt of discomfort went up the merchant's arm. He let go and the staff clattered to the deck.

Marsyas laughed and stuck out his tongue.

'You piece of goat shit!' yelled the merchant. 'Why don't you just fuck off back to where you come from?' Then he shut his mouth, because the stench was unbearable. And a moment later—perhaps it was the effect of that strange and extravagant brew of vapours and humours to which he had been exposed—something inside the merchant crumbled, and despair overwhelmed him. 'How miserable I am,' he said to himself. 'How unhappy! How desperate! Shackled to this burdensome world like a slave to a galley! Is this how my life is going to end—in a flea-bitten port far from home, poisoned by a satyr's fart?'

The Phoenician's legs gave way and he crumpled into a heap on the deck and blubbed like a child.

Marsyas smiled and inched closer. He reached out a tentative hand and laid it on the merchant's shoulder. The trader did not push it away. 'There,' Marsyas soothed, 'there, there, there. It's all right. There, there, there . . .' Marsyas nestled closer to him. The satyr kissed the merchant's neck and cheeks. He licked the tears from out of the merchant's eyes with the end of his pink tongue. The merchant's nostrils were filled with the overpowering stench of goat. At the back of his mind he could sense, as if far off, the thought that he should resist. But there was no resistance in him. He was soft as clay.

He leaned into the satyr's embrace. A quarter moon hung low over the sea, the wine-dark water shot through with cold silver light. Marsyas muttered endearments and ran his hand over the merchant's chest, down to his belly, towards his groin and down the inside of his legs, tickling the merchant in his tendermost places.

When the merchant looked into the goatling's eyes, he realised he was in love. He closed his eyes, and surrendered to the pleasure of it.

9

The merchant woke the following morning, disentangled himself from the arms of the satyr, and set about mustering a crew of strong-armed oarsmen and a capable helmsman to convey his new love to Lakedaimonia.

They cast off before noon, the oarsmen pulling against the force of the tide. They rowed steadily, cutting the water with practised skill. When they were clear of the harbour, they turned the boat and raised the sails, so that the soft wind could speed her across the ocean. Then the oarsmen rested.

In the bows of the boat, Marsyas and the merchant were resting too, nestled in each other's arms on a pile of sheepskins, like young lovers who had only just discovered the pleasures of love. When night fell, they gazed up at the stars, drinking wine in which they dunked chunks of the peasant bread, flavoured with the honey, for which Miletos was famed.

At the stern, with only the leaping porpoises for company, the helmsman stood alone with his hand on the tiller, watching the moon and the chill stars that hung over the sea.

The sea was a dead calm, the winds steady, gentle and warm upon the skin. At each touch of Marsyas's fingers, the merchant thought his heart would burst with joy. The Phoenician had, in his years as a sailor, enjoyed countless nights in the arms of different lovers. He knew how they made love in Asia Minor and Africa. He had lingered with girls and with boys, the young and the old, the male and the female and the hermaphrodite, the tall and the squat, the thin and the fat, and the shy and the passionate. Believing that he knew all there was to know of desire, he had resigned himself to the weariness that descends upon the act of love when, finally, there is nothing more to be known. But this satyr was a revelation. The merchant felt like a boy of fifteen again, tasting love for the first time.

'Oh,' he moaned as gazed into Marsyas's eyes, 'my sweet love! Let's live together in Arkadia! Let's be together eternally . . .'

The boat scudded westwards on the brisk winds. The helmsman held firmly to the tiller. The oarsmen slept the sleep of those who know what it is to do an honest day's work. Meanwhile Marsyas and the Phoenician engaged in amorous games until late in the night. They slept, they woke, they ate, they made love, and then they slept and woke and ate and made love again. Thus the hours passed.

On the third night of their voyage, when they were almost half way across the ocean, having enjoyed a strong following wind, Marsyas woke suddenly. He sat upright and looked about him. Something had woken him, some kind of sound. He padded to the stern where the helmsman was standing. 'Something woke me,' he said. 'Did you hear what it was?'

With the unruffled calm of a man who had spent years of his life at sea, and who was unsurprised by just about everything, the helmsman shrugged, 'I think somebody is singing.'

'Where?' asked Marsyas.

'Out there,' said the helmsman, pointing towards the dark, flat ocean where there was nothing but the endless swaying of the waves.

Marsyas listened.

The voice came again. It was the sound of a man singing with a voice of such sweet intensity that Marsyas felt a sharp stab of jealousy. He padded back amidships and leaned over the rail of the boat. The voice came closer. Soon Marsyas was able to make out the words. It sounded as if they came from the undulating waves themselves.

Though the ocean's choppy motion
is soon stilled by my sweet singing,
there's no balm or salve or lotion
that can keep the salt from stinging.

Marsyas peered across the dark water. The singing became louder, more distinct. As it did so, the helmsman let go of the tiller, overcome by the beauty of the music. The boat turned into the wind and settled, bobbing on the surface of the water, sails flapping and snapping. The helmsman hunched in the stern and started to sob.

The merchant grunted in his sleep but did not stir.

The voice became louder. Marsyas leaned out as far as he dared.

For the fish they bite and nibble
at my lacerated flesh,

and it doesn't take a Sibyl
to imagine the distress.

Oh, those savage Thracian women—
how I wish I'd stayed in Hades!
How I hate this endless swimming—
torn apart by crazy ladies.

In the pale light of the quarter moon, Marsyas could see something bobbing along on the surface of the waters. It was about the size of a large melon, half dark and half bright. When it drifted closer on the tide, Marsyas saw that it was the head of a youth with tousled hair and fine features. The mouth opened and closed as the head sang the sweetest, most exquisite music.

Marsyas looked closer. The head was not attached to any body. Instead it was truncated at the neck in a tangled mess of sinew and tendon. Yet still it sang, ascending and descending the scale as it went—now up, now down—on the water's surface.

Marsyas was fascinated. 'Who are you?' he whispered.

The singing stopped. By now, the head was almost knocking against the sides of the bireme, just out of reach. There was a pause. 'I am Orpheus, son of Oiagros,' it said. 'And who are you, brave voyager?'

The satyr leaned over to take a closer look. 'You know what?' he said, 'I think that might make us brothers. My name's Marsyas. Also son of Oiagros. Or of Hyagnis, or of Olympos, or of some other fucker.'

'Marsyas,' the head replied. 'I know you! I knew you when you were a little orphaned satyr kid in the cradle, and I was tutor in music to Midas. Why are you crossing the dark ocean?'

'I'm off to find something,' Marsyas said. He wasn't sure he wanted to tell Orpheus everything just yet. 'My friend Dionysos . . .'

At the mention of Dionysos, the head of Orpheus gurgled strangely. Marsyas stopped mid-sentence and took a closer look. He could see that the eyes were wide with fear.

'You are a friend of Dionysos?' the head whispered. 'Is Dionysos on the boat?'

'No. He's in India. Or somewhere. Why?'

'And *women*?' Again, the question was hushed. 'Are there any *women* on board?'

'What do you have against women?' asked Marsyas. He settled down on the deck and propped his chin on his folded arms, resting on the railing. It was fun talking to Orpheus. He started to prepare himself for a good, long conversation.

'Promise me there are no women.'

'I promise.'

Just then, a stray wave lapped into the open mouth, and the head of Orpheus spluttered.

'By the way, brother,' Marsyas said, 'you don't look in great shape. What happened to the rest of you?'

'The bakkhai,' the head of Orpheus said.

Marsyas frowned. 'The who?'

'Dionysos's women.'

Marsyas did not remember Dionysos mentioning any women. 'What did they do to you?' he asked.

'They tore me to shreds. They ripped my head clean apart from my body,' the head said.

'You must have annoyed them.'

'I spurned their love.'

'Well, serves you right,' Marsyas said. 'A satyr would never spurn *anyone's* love, which is probably why I still have my head. You're lucky they didn't do worse.'

'Oh!' the head of Orpheus cried, 'But if that were the extent of my misfortune, I would be a lucky man indeed. For my lovely Eurydike remains in the kingdom of Hades, whilst I float through Poseidon's vast territories.'

The satyr's cock twitched. 'Eurydike?' he asked, leering into the dark water. 'A pretty name. Was she good? I mean, did she give you a good going over?'

A sigh came from below. 'Friend Marsyas,' the head of Orpheus said, 'if you could have set eyes upon her, you would have wept with joy. Her love was pure, beyond all carnality.'

'No wonder she got fed up with you,' Marsyas said. Poets always went on about purity and truth when all they wanted to do, like everybody else, was to poke themselves into some warm hole and jiggle themselves around a bit.

But then the head let out a cry of sorrow, and Marsyas took pity on the poor thing. 'You say you lost her,' he said. 'How?'

'Ah,' said the head. 'Pursued by the god Aristaeus, she chose death over shame. She was bitten by a snake and she descended into Hades. And then I, Orpheus, went to fetch her.'

Marsyas leaned out over the side. He was impressed, despite himself. 'You went to *Hades*? How did you get there?'

'Somewhere in Thrace,' the head said, 'in a place where the pine trees grow as thickly as a man's beard, there is a stream that plunges into the earth through a deep crevice. If you dare to enter, you will find a way that leads down to Hades's court. Few men have made the journey, and even fewer have returned. This was the difficult road I trod in search of my Eurydike.'

'But you messed up,' Marsyas said.

The head of Orpheus rolled its eyes. 'Yes,' it said sadly. 'I messed up.'

The two of them fell silent. Marsyas could hear the slap, slap, slap of the waves against the bows of the boat, the merchant's snoring, and the occasional sob from the helmsman at the stern.

Then the satyr had a thought. It was a thought that, if it worked out, would save him a lot of trouble. After all, he reasoned, it might not be that his voice was *bad*. It might simply be that it was *untutored*. 'Tell me, Orpheus,' he said, 'where are you heading?'

'Lesbos,' the head of Orpheus said. 'If I know the winds and the tides, that is where they are carrying me.'

'What if I were to fish you out?' suggested Marsyas. 'You could teach me how to sing, and in exchange we could find a way to get your head stuck back onto some kind of body.'

'A poet's greatness,' the head said piously, 'lies in not refusing destiny, but instead in embracing it. It is thus that the poet's spirit soars above the harshness of necessity.'

Marsyas sighed. Poets were difficult. You had to know how to deal with them. 'Destiny is all very well,' he said, 'but tell me, Orpheus, do the fish nibble at you?'

The eyes rolled in their sockets, white flashes in the darkness. 'Why, yes, they do, for I have no hands to fight them off. But I sing to calm them, and when they hear me sing, they nibble less.'

'What about the salt? Does it sting your wounds?'

'Indeed,' the head conceded, 'it burns me like fire.'

'And can your singing move the ocean to saltlessness?'

'Alas, no! If I can seduce the fish and the stones and the

trees, it is because in so doing I do not betray their nature. A tree that follows the sound of my voice is merely a tree that follows the sound of my voice. A fish that stops nibbling at the entrails hanging from my neck is only a fish that no longer nibbles. But an ocean without salt is no ocean at all. For this reason, I cannot seduce the ocean to saltlessness.'

Marsyas nodded. 'And your eyes?' he said. 'I see that they are red. Are they painful?'

'If they burn,' the head of Orpheus replied, 'it is in part because of the briny ocean, and in part because of the savage bitterness of my tears.' The poet's eyes misted over, his soul elevated on the swelling tide of his own lyricism.

'Hmmm,' said Marsyas. 'And what about your skin? If you don't mind me saying, it's looking a bit puffy.'

'That, I cannot deny. Once my skin was soft and smooth, but the waters have caused it to pucker and fold.'

'You can be nice and dry here on the deck,' Marsyas said. 'We've got olives, wine, the bread of Miletos, drenched in honey. . . . . .'

The eyes seemed to soften a little. 'Oh, the tender bread of Miletos!' the head whispered.

Marsyas reached down and took a boat hook from the deck—a long pole at the end of which was a finely fashioned bronze claw, like the claw of an eagle. 'Of course,' he said, 'if you are not interested, if you have poetry and destiny and things to worry about, I can just take this pole here and shove you back out to sea.'

'No,' said the head. 'Please. Just a little bread.'

'And destiny?' Marsyas asked. 'What about destiny, Orpheus?'

'Destiny can wait. Please—bring me in, Marsyas,' the head said.

Marsyas hooked the bronze claw around the head's tangled locks. He twirled the pole a couple of times so that the hair held firm. Then Marsyas lifted the head of Orpheus out of the sea. It was surprisingly heavy.

Marsyas hauled it in. Then he set it down upon the deck, unwrapping the skeins of hair from the eagle's claw.

10

Marsyas propped the severed head of Orpheus on top of a coil of rope. The boat continued to drift. The merchant snored and turned in his sleep. Back in the stern, the helmsman went on sobbing.

'Now,' Marsyas said, sitting back on his haunches, 'let's get started.'

'How about some wine first?' suggested the poet's head. 'I'm parched. Or perhaps you could give me a piece of the bread of Miletos?'

Marsyas looked at the head coldly. 'A true poet is concerned with art before food,' he said.

The head of Orpheus sighed. Above them the constellations twinkled—the leaping dolphin, the broad-winged swan. The moon cast a thin light over the waters.

'If you're not going to give me wine, at least give me fresh water,' the head said.

Marsyas poured some water from an urn into the upturned mouth. It trickled out a few inches lower, where the neck had been severed. The head seemed satisfied. 'Ready?' it asked.

The satyr nodded.

'The first thing to understand,' the head said, 'is that the study of music begins with five years of listening. Then you must endure five years of solitude and silence. Next you must suffer five years of intensive practice, during which you eschew wine and love and all other pleasure.'

Up in the bows of the boat, the Phoenician merchant stirred in his sleep. He propped himself up on one elbow, eyes half open, and blearily took in the scene. He saw the satyr, his love, conversing with a severed head on the deck. But in his mind the soothing voice reason reassured him he was only dreaming. The merchant lay down once more and resumed his snoring.

Marsyas looked at the head sceptically. 'Fifteen years?' he asked.

'Yes,' said the head.

'What about the short version?'

'There's no short version. You satyroi are so impatient. That is why there are many great men in the world, but there has never been a single great satyr.'

Marsyas leaned forwards and bared his teeth. Then he picked up the head so that they were eye-to-eye. 'Orpheus,' he growled, 'think of the nibbling of the fish. Think of the salt that chews at your flesh. You don't want me to throw you back and go fishing for a better teacher do you?'

The head was terrified. 'Put me down!' it shrieked. 'Put me down. Let's talk about it.'

Marsyas did not put the head down. 'How long will it take?'

'Perhaps a week for the basics.'

'Too long.' Marsyas dangled the head towards the gently lapping waves.

'Three days?' the head spluttered.

'You might as well ask for eternity.'

'A single night, then!' the head said. 'I'll teach you the art of music in a single night!'

Marsyas paused and thought for a few seconds. Then he grinned and he returned the head to the coiled rope. 'That's better,' he said. 'A night will do it. Now, let me give you some of that wine.'

The satyr reached for the wine jar, poured a libation into the open mouth, watching it seep out of the neck. He took a glug himself. The head seemed refreshed by the drink.

'Right,' Marsyas said. 'Let's get going. I want to be singing my first song by dawn.'

'We will begin with a little theory,' said the head of Orpheus. 'I will sing you a scale in the Mixolydian mode. Listen well.'

The head sang a scale, both ascending and descending, in the Mixolydian mode. And although it was only a head, unattached to lungs or throat, the music was sweet and clear. The merchant turned over on the deck where he lay. Tears appeared on his cheeks. At the stern, the sobbing of the helmsman continued.

But Marsyas was unimpressed. The Mixolydian failed to touch him. 'Sing something else,' he said.

The head of Orpheus frowned. 'Though the Mixolydian is beautiful,' the head said, 'some claim it enervates the mind. Let me sing the Dorian instead. The Dorian makes the mind moderate and settled.'

Then Orpheus sang a scale in the Dorian. The soft swell of the sea subsided. What clouds there were—ribbons of vapour drifting across the face of the thin moon—scudded to the horizon and were gone. The night held its breath.

Marsyas was unmoved. 'I don't like it,' he said. He drew back his lips to reveal his teeth. 'Try another.'

The head of Orpheus thought for a while, then its mouth opened again to sing another scale. Immediately, Marsyas was enraptured. His face softened. Tears welled in the corners of his eyes.

In the bows, the Phoenician merchant was dreaming. He dreamed he was a bee drunk on honey. He dreamed of the shuddering of tens of thousands of pairs of wings. He dreamed of the hum and throb of the hive.

Hearing the music, Marsyas felt an ache in his heart for Kybele. 'Wonderful!' he cried. 'Wonderful! Tell me, what mode is this?'

'It is the Phrygian,' the head said. 'It is said to inspire enthusiasm.'

'Sing it again,' said Marsyas.

'Do not waste your time on the Phrygian,' said the head. 'It is a barbarian mode.'

Marsyas leaned forwards until he was almost nose-to-nose with the head. 'Call it what you like, but this is the one I want. Sing it again, or I'll throw you back.'

The head of Orpheus, terrified of the sting of the salt water, did as it was asked.

'Good,' said Marsyas. 'Now sing the same thing, but this time descending.'

The head obliged.

'And up again.'

Orpheus's head sang back up the scale.

'Now do it both up and down with some twiddly bits in the middle—'

The head of Orpheus sang, both up and down the Phrygian scale, with some twiddly bits in the middle.

The merchant's dream became more elaborate. He was no longer a bee. Instead he was a king. He was seated on a throne amidst a cloud of bees, and he feasted upon a blackened honeycomb charred by burning in the fire. The honeycomb was sweet and bitter. His crown was lopsided on his head, his eyes red with sleeplessness. A bearskin was draped over his shoulders. His beard was sticky with honey.

Below decks, the oarsmen stirred. They started to shout in confusion. The helmsman, hearing their bewildered cries, hurried below deck to calm them.

'Now you try,' the head of Orpheus said to the satyr. 'Start with the first note. When you get that right, we can move on to the second. Once we have the entire scale, we will do it ascending, then descending. Finally we can work on the ornamentation. That should take us until dawn.'

The Phoenician merchant made a sound in his sleep. It was not a quite a snore, but instead something else, a thrumming, an apian buzzing.

Marsyas composed himself, listening as the head of Orpheus sang.

'*Laaaaa—*'

The note lingered on the breeze.

The satyr closed his eyes. He shivered with pleasure and held the note in his head. Then he opened his mouth to sing.

The merchant dreamed of blackness, of soot, of honey, of charcoal. He dreamed of rustling wings and waxy honeycomb. He was a merchant dreaming he was a king dreaming he was a bee dreaming he was a merchant. Servants brought jars of honey and laid them before his throne. In each jar, staring out of the golden liquid, was the head of a woman; and each of the women he recognised: a slave girl he had violated; a woman he had tricked into sharing his bed with the promise of marriage, only to abscond the following day; an African girl so determined to resist his advances he had thrown her overboard into the Aegean. Jar after jar, each one a head bearing a face he had thought forgotten. They stared, perfect in the honey preserve, eyes wide, mouths gaping. The buzzing of bees became louder. The bitter taste of burnt honeycomb filled his mouth.

Marsyas looked at the head of Orpheus. His teacher raised an eyebrow. 'Now it is your turn,' the head said.

Then Marsyas started to sing.

'*Maaaeee . . .*'

It was the same note as that sung by Orpheus. Yet it was not the same note. The sound was cracked and jagged, harsh on the ears.

The merchant's dream lurched. The heads stirred in their jars and rose to the surface. Their lips parted, honey-drenched, and uttered words of desire. 'Kiss me,' they said. 'Kiss me, my sweet, like you did before.'

'. . . *maaaeee . . . maaaeee . . .*' Marsyas sang.

Through the palace windows swarmed ten thousand bees, black like smoke. They crawled into the merchant's nose, his mouth, his ears. They clustered on his eyelids. They jabbed him with barbed stings.

The merchant woke with a scream and scrambled to his feet, the dream still upon him.

Marsyas held the note, eyes closed, concentrating hard: '*maaaeee . . . maaaeee . . .*'

The merchant staggered. He cried out in agony. Blood burst from his eardrums. Marsyas felt that surge of joy which is known only to true artists.

'*maaaeee . . . maaaeee . . .*'

The waves churned, becoming restless, tossing the boat here and there. Below deck the oarsmen and the helmsmen cried out in terror.

'*maaaeee . . . maaaeee . . .*'

On Marsyas's face, an expression of ecstasy.

The Phoenician merchant put his hands to his ears, feeling warm dampness of blood. He held his palms in front of him. They were dark in the moonlight. An incessant buzzing filled his head. His skull was a living hive. Every thought was a bee.

Then the merchant remembered how, when he had been a boy, his father had taken him walking on the hills close to the hives, and told him that, should he ever anger the bees, he could only save himself by plunging into some great body of water.

The Phoenician staggered to the side of the boat. He looked down at the dark waves.

'*maaaeee . . . maaaeee . . .*'

The merchant plunged over the side.

'*maaaeee . . . maaaeee . . .*'

The moon hid behind a wreath of cloud. Cold winds tore at the bireme. The boat bucked and shuddered, bows plunging downwards, then lifting to the sky.

'*maaaeee . . . maaaeee . . .*'

Marsyas felt his breath giving out. And he did not even notice when an object the size of a large melon toppled from where it had been propped on a coil of rope, rolled across the deck, and went tumbling out of the boat to fall back into the dark waters.

'*maaaeee . . .*

'. . . he . . . he . . .
'heee . . .'

Marsyas was done. He opened his eyes and looked round. The head of Orpheus was gone. So, too, was the merchant. From below deck came a terrible wailing. The moon was trembling in fear behind the clouds. The waves started to subside.

Marsyas looked over the side. 'Orpheus?' he yelled across the ocean. 'Where did you go? Tell me—how did I do?'

As the sea returned to a flat calm, the moon emerged from the clouds. In the stillness, Marsyas could hear Orpheus's voice, a long way off, raised in sweet and mournful song.

Oh, those savage Thracian women—
how I wish I'd stayed in Hades!
How I hate this endless swimming—
torn apart by crazy ladies.

'How did I do?' Marsyas called again. 'How did I do?'

But Orpheus did not reply, and in a few moments his honey-sweet voice dwindled to nothing.

11

The following morning, the sails were full again, and Marsyas and the crew were gathered by the stern. Marsyas chatted amicably with the helmsman as they munched on olives, honey-bread and wine. Nobody had been particularly sad to see the Phoenician go. Now they had the boat to themselves, the hired hands decided that they might as well keep it that way and, living equitably and in harmony, engage in a spot of piracy for a living. They volunteered to take Marsyas to the Lakedaimonian coast, grateful that he had liberated them from their onerous employment. As they chatted, the boat cut through the brilliant seas. By the time the sun was at its zenith, they sighted land.

They moored in a little cove, a natural harbour. There they put Marsyas ashore, thanking him for his kindness in helping them rid themselves of the merchant. Marsyas hopped onto the beach. He gave them a farewell wave, scampered into the trees, and was gone.

Once he had gone a little way into the forest, Marsyas paused and sniffed the air to get his bearings. Against the salt taste of the sea, he could smell, drifting from the north, the sweetness of late pollen, the mustiness of leaf mould and the richness of swelling fruit. It was the scent of the encroaching autumn. He felt goatishly happy, and skipped a little dance of joy. Then he sniffed the air again, and headed inland from the sea, following his nose, making his way towards the line of green, wooded hills in the distance. The ground was soft underfoot. The sunlight was scattered into a thousand parts by the leaves of the trees, a cascade of emerald light.

Soon Marsyas became hungry: for food, for company, and, above all, for love. The inept fumblings of the Phoenician merchant had served their purpose, but he wanted something more, something light and refined. He wanted the gossamer love of a nymph.

He heard their laughter first, almost indistinguishable from the trickling and tinkling of the countless streams as they tumbled down from the distant mountain peaks. He pricked up his goat's ears and looked about him, but saw nothing. The laughter continued. The satyr's cock twitched.

He came into a small glade. He was certain now that he could smell them. The trees and bushes rustled in the breeze. There were strange flickerings of light at the edges of his vision. *How many are there?* he wondered. *Two, three, four?* Marsyas's cock rose, tasting the air with its blind snout.

There is nothing a nymph likes more than a game of hide-and-seek. Marsyas put his nose to the ground and his nostrils flared, drinking in the scents of air and soil. *I'll find you*, he thought. He sniggered to himself with anticipated lust.

The nymphs were keeping upwind of him. The soft mockery of their laughter came now from here, now from there. He crept through the undergrowth, tracking them, sometimes on two legs like a man, sometimes on four like a goat. He followed the fleet-footed maidens by their laughs, by the rustling of leaves, by the imprint of their heels and toes in the soft, mossy ground. He clambered over tree trunks and boulders. He peeked through the branches, hardly daring to breathe.

Then he saw them. There were four of them in all, standing in a clearing by the banks of a small, burbling stream. They were laughing and whispering behind the backs of their hands, dressed in light garments that made them seem more naked than would nakedness alone. One of them was short and full-bodied. Her long, wet hair fell down her back in great tumbling curls. Her cheeks and her lips were full. Another was thin and pale as a poplar. The seriousness of her expression was both sad and exciting. A third was neither tall nor short, but she had a smile of sun-like radiance. The fourth was shy, or pretended to be. Her skin was the colour of olives. Her back was turned. Marsyas could see the line of her spine, a curve beneath her thin linen robe. He gazed hungrily at her long legs and the fullness of her buttocks.

Then the satyr stepped into the sunlight and bleated in greeting. His beautiful fur was covered with burrs, but he did not care. The nymphs feigned surprise, shrieking and darting to the riverbank. Marsyas gave a small bow. Three of the nymphs slipped off their linen garments. Backs turned, they threw Marsyas coy looks over their shoulders before diving into the stream. They were gone in a moment, dissolved in the sparkling waters, leaving only one behind, the shortest of the three. She beckoned to Marsyas, laid him down on the grass, and kissed him on the mouth. Then she picked off his burrs, one by one. When she had rid him of them all, she held him to the ground with one hand, and used the other to tickle him in all the places that he liked. She perched on top of his pink and naked belly, reaching up to pull down long skeins of ivy from the trees. Marsyas put his hands behind his head and watched as she wove the ivy into two crowns. She placed one upon his horns and the other she sat on her own forehead. Thus crowned, the nymph let him remove the cloth in which she was wrapped. 'What is your name?' she asked.

'I'm Marsyas. What are you called?'

'Shhh!' she said, and put her finger to his lips.

When she was perfectly naked, they performed a number of acts so startlingly pleasurable that Marsyas believed he might burst with joy. They exchanged caresses, kisses, endearments, touches as light as a spiderweb. They tickled, prodded and nibbled. They sighed with pleasure, hooted and shrieked with laughter, tussled in the glorious sunlight, goat body and nymph body, delicious and carefree.

By sunset, they were both exhausted. The nymph lay on her back with her chest rising-falling, cheeks flushed. Marsyas lay by her side, drenched in sweat, panting, letting out small, involuntary bleats, the stench of horny goat on him. The ivy crowns had fallen from their heads. Marsyas picked one of them up and put it on the nymph's beaded brow. They kissed.

Night fell. The moon came out and the nymph began to shiver. She reached for her linen robe. Marsyas watched as she wrapped herself once again. When she was dressed, she leaned over and bit him upon the ear. She inserted her tongue into the coiled flesh until he giggled with delight.

Then the nymph stood up and went down to the water's edge. Her footsteps were silent in the moonlight. From a basket hidden in the reeds she took out a hunk of bread, a flask of wine, some dried olives, and a plump quince. She wrapped these things in a piece of cloth and tossed them to the satyr. He caught the bundle. Then she plunged into the waters and was gone.

By tomorrow she would have forgotten him; already she could not remember the little satyr's name.

Marsyas ate alone and in silence. How sweet the nymph had been. He wondered about the others, how differently they might have kissed, what pleasures they might have enjoyed all of them together. But the thought did not trouble him too much. Sometimes one, sometimes two, sometimes four, he thought: what does it matter, if there is pleasure?

After he had finished the feast, Marsyas licked his fingers clean. Then he scampered off up the bank and into the forest, negotiating the Arkadian rocks with the dexterity only possible in one who is part goat.

12

Marsyas rambled over the hillsides by moonlight. As he went, he hummed to himself and chatted with passing goats. When the night became cold, he found lodgings with an old shepherd. The two of them huddled under blankets in the shepherd's hut, staring into the flames of the little wood fire, enjoying the brotherly communion of rustics who have no need to speak to each other, because life is simple and there is nothing to convey. The wind blew through the trees some way off. An owl hooted on the hillside. The taste of the nymph lingered on Marsyas's tongue. Fleeting thoughts passed through his mind, but he did not grasp after them, because there is never any need to grasp after thoughts. Whether you remember or forget, the seasons still turn on their axis, night still becomes day and day becomes night. There will always be another nymph with a carefree laugh and a touch as light as the spring breeze. There will always be fresh cheese to eat. There will always be farmers offering hospitality and baked bread to the weary traveller. There will always be shepherds willing to share their solitary huts and the crackling of their fires with a stranger, and not because every stranger might be a god in disguise, but merely because every stranger is a stranger, and who, in a strange land, would not wish for a warm place to sleep? These things are immutable truths.

The owl hooted again. The satyr snuggled deeper into his blanket, hugging his knees. Sleep came quickly.

The following morning the two of them breakfasted in silence. When they had finished, Marsyas turned to the shepherd. 'I'm looking for a reed pipe,' he said.

It was the first thing that either had said. The shepherd thought for a while, looking at the cold embers of the fire. 'There's plenty of them reeds down by the stream,' he said. 'Take one of them. They're easy to whittle.'

'The reed I'm looking for is different,' said Marsyas. 'It belonged to the goddess Athene.'

The shepherd turned to look at him with rheumy eyes. 'I don't go mucking with the gods,' he said, 'and the gods don't come mucking with me.'

Marsyas shrugged and thanked the shepherd. Then he left to resume his wanderings.

Marsyas wandered through Arkadia as if through a dream of paradise. He lay in beautiful valleys carpeted with flowers, the sun caressing his belly. He flirted and tumbled with nymphs. He shared the company of his brother satyroi and seilenoi. And sometimes he remembered to ask about the aulos. But, as the old saying goes, it is a difficult thing to find an aulos in Arkadia, and it is hard for a satyr to keep a single thing in mind. So for much of the time, Marsyas was distracted, lost in pleasure, forgetting why it was he was there.

As the autumn wore on, the trees shed their leaves, turning the forest floor the colour of bronze. Then one morning

Marsyas woke to see the early light over the mountains scattered by the mist, and he thought of Kybele. All of a sudden, he ached to be home in Phrygia. He thought of the aulos and how his search, half distracted though it had been, had proved fruitless. Then he thought of how the goddess would mock him if he were to return empty handed. There was nothing to be done about it, he consoled himself. He was sad to be returning without the aulos, but at least he had tried. He had asked a couple of people, looked around a bit. He couldn't have done more. So the little satyr started to make his way back to the coast. As he went, he wove together elaborate strings of excuses with which he might explain his ineptitude to the Goddess.

But, destiny being what it is, in the end it was not Marsyas who found the aulos. Instead it was the aulos that found Marsyas. One chilly autumn morning, when he was not far from the coast, and was curled up asleep in the arms of a nymph, he opened his eyes to the sound of excited chattering.

It was a band of satyroi, presided over by a pot-bellied seilenos. Marsyas sat up, rubbing his eyes. The satyroi greeted him with the yelps and bleats customary among their kind, and they ogled the nymph, who gathered up her diaphanous robe to cover herself.

When the greetings were over, the pot-bellied seilenos spoke. He had heard, he said, that Marsyas was looking for an instrument formed out of a double reed. Some time ago, he had stumbled upon just such a thing in the care of a certain shepherd, who had been glad to be rid of it. The seilenos lifted up a coarsely woven bag. 'I have it with me,' he said. 'Would you like it?'

He rummaged in the bag and drew out a pair of reeds,

joined together to form a double pipe, pierced through with holes. He handed the instrument over to Marsyas.

The little satyr turned it over in his hands, his lower lip trembling. 'Can I try it?' he asked.

'Certainly. Not a single one of us could make it work,' the seilenos said. 'You may have more luck.'

Marsyas put the pipes to his lips and blew. At first the only sound was a high-pitched squawk.

'You see our point,' the seilenos said. 'It's useless.'

Marsyas thought hard, examining the aulos closely. Then he put it to his lips again. He filled his lungs, pressed his lips to the mouthpiece, and let out the air slowly and steadily. This time the sound was as sweet as honey. The satyroi sat back in astonishment. The nymph gasped with delight.

Marsyas let the note linger. Then he removed the pipes from his lips.

There was silence, and then an excited jabbering. The seilenos leaned forward. 'How did you do that?' he asked.

'I just blew it.'

'Well, none of us could make it work. I don't know why not,' said the seilenos. 'Can't say I care for it myself. Do you want it?'

Marsyas nodded.

'Well it's yours,' the paunchy little fellow said roughly, 'because I'm buggered if I know how to use it. But there is a price.'

'A price?'

A hungry desire appeared in the seilenos's eyes. He glanced at the nymph. 'If she is willing, of course,' he said, giving the girl a wink.

She smiled. 'I can be persuaded,' she replied. 'And I'm not

going to get much more out of this Phrygian now he has his new toy to play with . . .'

Hearing this, the satyroi cheered. The seilenos and nymph joined hands, and the satyroi, as if celebrating some marriage rite, formed a circle around them. Then they sang a little song that made the nymph skip with delight:

A flute you cannot tootle
is a rather useless tool:
there's no point in a pipe you cannot play!

So let Marsyas the musician
take his solitary pleasure—
we'd rather have a nymph-girl any day.

There's nothing wrong with music—
it is good to hum a tune;
we wouldn't want to criticise the art:

but solitary piping
is a sad and tragic thing
when a nymph is keen to play the treble part.

When the song was done, they all of them fell into a giggling heap—the satyroi, the seilenos and the nymph. By the time they had picked themselves up, Marsyas had already scuttled off into the forest with his aulos.

13

Marsyas made his way up to a quiet cave in the hills. There he sat down on his haunches, put the aulos to his lips, and started to play. The music came naturally, without any strain. He did not worry about any Mixolydian this and Dorian that and Phrygian the other. Instead, Marsyas breathed through the flute as if the instrument were an extension of his heart and of his longing. He played the way he fucked, without a clear plan, fully immersed in the ebb and the flow of things, unaware of anything other than rhythm, melody, texture, surprise, delight. And it was so easy. As he played, Marsyas thought about the absurdities of Orpheus's pedantic lessons. Music, he thought, could no more be made from such dross than could a good, tasty stew be fashioned from goat turds. All the satyr had to do was close his eyes and let the music guide him. His lips knew how to move of themselves. His fingers knew how to take up their positions on the twin shafts of the pipes. Music thrilled through his body as easily as a stream tumbles down from a mountain peak.

He played and played and played, and his skin trembled with pleasure. The sun arced across the sky and fell towards the earth. It set in a blaze of reds and pinks, and the moon rose. Marsyas put down his flute. He had not given a thought to anything else since the morning. He had not eaten, had not drunk anything, had not even thought of the nymph with whom he had shared the previous night.

His belly was rumbling, but he had no energy left to forage, so he decided to go without. Who needed food when there was music? Now, he said to himself, he would sleep. And tomorrow he would show the world what he could do with his aulos.

With this comforting thought, Marsyas—his little furred limbs clasped around the pipe as if it were the sweetest thing in the world—curled up in the mouth of the cave and closed his eyes to sleep.

The following morning he descended from the cave and found his way to a meadow filled with late flowering grasses. The meadow lay in a little valley upon whose gentle slopes shaggy pine trees jutted from the ridges of rambling rocks. In the middle of the meadow was a place where four roads converged, each leading to a different village and, beyond that, to trading routes that extended both landward and seaward. At the place where the four roads joined was a large boulder and propped on the boulder was a small basket of gifts, offerings to the goddess Hekate, guardian of crossing places. Hungry after a day of fasting, Marsyas opened up the basket. Inside was a pat of cheese, along with some honeyed sweets, and a small flask of wine. He hesitated for a moment. Then he reasoned that the crossroads of the world were many, and that Hekate was an old woman with poor eyesight, an enfeebled mind, and almost certainly no appetite. She would not miss one small basket.

Marsyas drank down the wine, guzzled the cheese, and finished off his breakfast with the honeyed sweets. Then he wiped his mouth with the back of his hand, tossed the basket to one side, and clambered up on top of the boulder, where he sat up on his haunches. It was a perfect spot.

The satyr put the aulos to his lips, and he blew. From the pipe came a single, pure, note. He held it as long as he could, until his lungs were empty of air. In that single note, he told himself, there was more beauty and longing than in ten thousand threnodies played on Apollo's lyre.

He played another note, then a third and then a fourth—followed by a fifth and again a sixth. After the sixth note, the phrase was finished, complete and perfect. Marsyas removed the pipes from his lips and opened his eyes.

In front of him was a small crowd. Such is always the way in the countryside. You think that you are alone. You think that you can get away with anything you like, that you can fuck amongst the bushes and pilfer crops and murder a stranger for the fun of it without ever being found out. But there is always somebody watching you. Nothing ever goes unobserved in the countryside. Murderers and lovers, if they are wise, carry out their business in the crowded city streets where nobody ever pays any attention, and not in the wilderness where, it is said, even the rocks and trees have eyes.

Marsyas looked at the peasants who clustered around the boulder. The crowd stared back. He played the notes again, in sequence, a phrase. The peasants were quivering, expectant, hopeful. Marsyas played another phrase. Then he quickened his pace. The audience started to sway. The sound of Marsyas's music was carried on the breeze, over the fields and the valleys. Far off, peasants working in the fields threw down their tools and came at a run, as if possessed by a strange, foreign god. Lovers, screwing each other in their rude huts, interrupted their exertions. They rolled off each other, captivated by the promise of greater pleasures, pulled on their tunics and ran towards the crossroads. Priests and oracles, engaged in solemn rites in their grubby little temples, bid their gods curt farewells—a rudeness for which several were later punished most horribly—and bustled in their robes out of the temple precincts. Old men and women, hobbling on sticks, found their feet blessed with new life as they came running. Dogs yelped, goats bleated, donkeys brayed and mounted each other. Young girls and boys joined hands and, breathless, fled the villages for the valley.

The music became more frenetic as the crowd mustered. They stamped their feet in abandon, waved their arms in the air, throwing off their peasant cares. '*Hoi!*' they shouted joyfully. '*Hoi! Hoi! Hai! Hoi! Hai!*' Hand in pudgy hand, ecstatic and united, stinking of the farm, the cattle-shed, the country wine-shop, the unwashed bed, they celebrated their ecstasy. They trampled the grass underfoot until there was nothing but bare earth remaining. They wheeled, cycled and flailed, as the goddess Eurynome had once danced at the beginning of creation.

Then came the satyroi. They scurried from their hiding places and groves, followed by the nymphs and dryads, eager to hear this new excitement. Slower than their younger brethren, the seilenoi with their wineskins and pot bellies puffed their way down the crags to listen. Red in the face, bulbous-nosed, hard-cocked, they rubbed themselves with pleasure to hear the strains of Marsyas's music. From the skies descended a phalanx of korybantes with flashing armour.

They danced upon the clouds and clashed their cymbals and their weapons. Manflesh, womanflesh, boyflesh, girlflesh, satyrflesh, godflesh, goatflesh: for a while everything was mixed and nothing was separate, and the valley was nothing other than a vortex of raised arms and jerking bodies, of jutting elbows and waggling chins, of breasts and cocks and cunts and bellies and arses and a thousand voices knotting and unknotting in ecstatic cry.

Marsyas was so deep in the music that he was barely aware of the dancers. His body thrilled with the surge and pulse of the melody. His toes curled. His eyes were tightly closed. He felt as if he might explode with joy. He played a high note and held it. The Arkadian villagers shuddered and jerked with pleasure. Marsyas felt the breath giving out in his lungs. The note faded until it was nothing at all.

Then there was silence.

A sigh rippled through the crowd. Marsyas opened his eyes. He looked down at the exhausted masses. Then he bleated with pleasure and held his pipes up towards the sky. 'Apollo,' he cried out, 'concede your crown. In the art of music, Marsyas is greatest.'

PART III
CONTEST

14

When Hermes arrived, on a whirring of tiny ankle-wings, his brother Apollo was gazing at himself in the polished bronze of a mirror, his torso like a shining pot. Beauty is not truth and truth is not beauty; but when Apollo looked in that bronzed mirror, it was with the belief that he was seeing both. He caught sight of Hermes in the mirror, no more than a blur, somewhere behind him. He placed the mirror down with a sigh. 'Brother Hermes,' he said. 'What brings you here? What do you have to tell?'

Hermes, youngest and most fleeting of gods, with the first down of youth still on his upper lip, only came to Apollo when he had news to pass on. God of transitions and crossings, he traded in that most weightless of commodities: information. He made it his business to know everything worth knowing; and because information is without heaviness, Hermes could slip between worlds, carrying great cargoes as if they were nothing at all.

Hermes had heard news of Marsyas's challenge, and the satyr's boldness had pricked his interest. He knew that Apollo would be angry, but in matters of music, Hermes bore a certain animus both towards Apollo and towards the race of satyrs. So here, he judged, there might be the opportunity to have some fun.

Hermes's resentment was deep-rooted. It went back to the day of his birth. The little god had been born of the nymph Maia, who lived in a cave on Mount Kyllene. He was a precocious child, born with all his faculties intact. On the day of his birth he ventured out of the mouth of the cave and saw a curious thing. Stones were scattered here and there across the hillside, but one stone amongst all the rest was *moving*, waddling along the mountain path. Fascinated by the moving stone, the infant Hermes crawled after it. He picked it up, flipped it upside down and found the underside soft. Four legs and a head drew themselves into the shell. Hermes giggled. Then he brought the thing—it was only later he learned it was not a stone, but was instead a 'tortoise'—crashing down on a rock, turning its soft parts to pulp. He scooped out the broken body with a sharp stone and threw away the mess of flesh and sinew. But he kept the shell.

First he made the shell into a boat which he floated upon the stream. Then he tried using the carapace as a hat. The hat, however, was too large and kept slipping from his head. Experimentally, he peed into it to see what it would do, but the piss just gathered in the shell, a little lake. The experiment proved inconclusive, so he emptied the shell out, washed it in the stream and stowed it away in the cave, convinced that it might one day be useful. Then he went off to explore the rest of the world.

By the afternoon, he had crawled his way to Pieria, where Apollo had his herds of cattle, ten thousand horned beasts milling about with udders full of milk. When he looked at the magnificent cattle, the child felt the sharp prickling of jealousy. *I want some*, he thought.

So Hermes stole fifty unblemished cattle, with fine horns and beautiful haunches, to use as playthings. To avoid leaving any trace or spoor, he put brushwood sandals of tamarisk and myrtle on his feet, and he drove the cattle backwards all the way to the cave on Mount Kyllene. Only one man, Battos by name, saw the theft. He was senile, tilling his vineyards and singing to himself, dribbling like a child. Hermes feared that Battos could not be trusted, or that his mouth would easily be loosened by forgetfulness or wine, so he turned the old man to stone. The symmetry of it was delightful: the day that had begun with a stone that came to life ended with a life that was turned to stone.

It was after dark when Hermes arrived with the cattle back at the cave. Maia scolded him for the theft, but she did not tell him to return the beasts. He was only a baby, an innocent. Who would think ill of him? Surely, she reasoned, Apollo would not miss fifty cattle from a herd of ten thousand.

But Apollo missed the beasts instantly. When the sun rose the following day, he cast his eyes over the fields of Pieria, and saw that fifty head of cattle were gone. No prints in the sand led away from the fields. There were no traces, no tracks. Furious, the god summoned a ragged troop of satyroi to assist him in recovering his property. He bribed the satyroi, offering them wine and food. And the little fuckers did a good job: they sniffed out the livestock by the smell of cow shit; and the trail led right to the mouth of Maia's cave.

But as Apollo and his band of trackers approached Mount Kyllene, they heard a strange sound, as haunting and delicate as the mountain mist. Apollo crept towards the mouth of the cave and peered inside. There he saw a baby, fresh-born, sitting up and serenading its mother, plucking at an extraordinary instrument. The body of the instrument was made from the shell of a tortoise stretched over with oxhide. Over the hide were stretched seven strings of cattle gut, secured with two great struts that Apollo instantly recognised as horns. Maia was sitting in the corner, watching her child play; and when little Hermes played an impressive scale passage, or a melody of particular sweetness, she clapped her hands together with delight.

Apollo recognised something familiar in the music: the mooing of calves, the sound of cattle bellowing to be milked, the din of slaughterhouse panic. He burst into the cave and snatched the instrument from his brother's lap. Hermes let out a cry, but when he saw the blazing anger in Apollo's eyes, he fell silent.

The god examined the instrument. He ran his fingers gently along the gut, making it thrum softly. He caressed the horns and stroked the skin. Hermes gurgled in a counterfeit of childish innocence. Apollo put down the lyre and picked up the baby. 'Where are the rest of them, you little shit-bag?' he hissed.

Hermes trembled.

'I know you did it,' Apollo said. 'Tell me you did it, or I will smash you to bits on the stone floor of this cave.'

'All right, Apollo,' Hermes said. 'I took them.'

'Where are they?'

Hermes started to sob as he pointed to the back of the cave. Then he lost control of his bowels, and he shat copiously. Apollo put him down in disgust. He stepped into the thick darkness at the back of the cave. He was greeted with lows of recognition as forty-nine amiable cattle sidled up to him. The god led them back out into the light. Then he turned to face his brother. 'You snot-nosed shit,' Apollo sighed. 'Keep the cows if you must. Take them all. Take the lot of them. I am sick of their stench. Be god of flocks and herds if you wish. But give me the lyre instead, and I will be god of music.'

Hermes, not daring to protest, gurgled in assent.

Apollo picked up the lyre and left, the rabble of satyroi following on behind.

Ever since then, Hermes had hated the satyroi, and had regarded his brother with deep jealousy. It pleased him to see Apollo slighted when it came to the art of music, and even more so to think that some Phrygian satyr might come off badly from the whole affair. So, a flurry of lightness and feathers, he fluttered over to Apollo and hovered just beside him.

'Speak, Hermes,' the god of music said.

Hermes smiled and drifted lightly to the ground. 'There is a certain satyr,' he said. 'His name is Marsyas . . .'

And Hermes told Apollo everything he knew.

When he had come to the end of his story, the messenger god fluttered backwards. He could see there was a deep fury brewing in his brother's mind.

'Frigging satyroi,' Apollo muttered. He rose to his feet and went towards the window to gaze over the valley. He could see the mountain slopes and the rolling hills that led all the way to Arkadia. 'Bring me my lyre,' Apollo said. 'I need soothing.'

Hermes scudded through the air to fetch the lyre from where it was hanging on a hook on the wall. He lifted it off the hook and carried it back, placing it in Apollo's hands. The god of music started to play, his fingers moving gently over the strings. Hermes listened with envy, head tilted on one side. Music for cattle: it had been a poor trade.

Having plucked a few sweet phrases to still his rage, Apollo put down his lyre and turned to his brother god. 'Hermes,' he said, 'take a message to this Phrygian satyr for me.'

Hermes's lip trembled, but he didn't protest.

'Tell him that the great god Apollo accepts his challenge. Invite him to a contest in Phrygia, so that we can decide who is greater in music. Appoint some judges. Let us have the Muses, and Tmolos the mountain god, and a couple of common peasants. Oh, and that halfwit king of Phrygia, Midas. Let us have him as well.'

'A contest?' Hermes said. 'What if you lose?'

'I will not lose, Hermes. I will win. And after I have won, I will take the fucker, and I will string him up, and I will slaughter him like a goat.'

The god Apollo turned away from the window. He sighed and hung his head. 'See to it, Hermes.'

With a buzzing of wings, like the sound of a passing dragonfly, the fleet-footed god was gone.

Apollo picked up his lyre and continued to play.

15

Were it not for the pot-bellied seilenos, Midas often told himself, none of this would have happened. Were it not for that old sot, and for the cruelty of Dionysos, he would still have a wife and a daughter. But when he thought back on the whole business, the thing that Midas found hardest to bear was this: he knew it was all his own fault.

The palace attendants had found the seilenos in the palace gardens some months before. The drunkard was asleep amongst the flowers. The attendants had wanted to drive him out with sticks and curses, but the king ordered that the seilenos be bound with wreaths of flowers and creeping plants. Thus garlanded, the seilenos was brought to Midas, who loosened the old fellow's bonds and welcomed him as a brother.

Midas had always had a strange affinity with the satyroi and seilenoi. Whilst he traced his ancestry through Gordios, lover of Kybele, there were others who said that his parentage was a more *goatish* affair. There were rumours that a passing satyr had spilled his seed into the goddess whilst she was sleeping, that Gordios was cuckolded, and that the son who succeeded the throne was not his own. Midas, for his own part, did not really know. But whilst he proclaimed himself son of Gordios, it was in the company of satyroi and seilenoi that he often felt happiest.

So Midas invited the seilenos to join with him in a feast. They feasted for five days, drunk on wine and conversation. And when the seilenos at last stood up to leave, in an attempt to detain him longer, Midas asked him a question. 'Friend seilenos,' he said, 'before you go, I have one final question to ask. You've shared much wisdom with me over these five days of feasting, and this final question will perhaps serve to draw together this wisdom, as a net draws together the many fish of the sea.'

'Of course, your majesty,' replied the seilenos.

Midas hesitated. 'Tell me, then,' he said. 'What is the greatest boon for mankind?'

The drunkard's eyes flashed with shrewd wisdom. 'Midas,' he smiled. 'Do not make me answer this. You will not thank me.'

Midas laughed. What could this little pot-bellied court-jester say that could be so very terrible? 'Tell me,' Midas repeated. 'What is the greatest boon?'

The seilenos looked him in the eye. 'What is best for man,' he said, 'is to have never been born.'

When the king met the seilenos's eyes, he saw they were grave and that the little old drunkard was drunk no longer. Midas shuddered. His throat went dry. 'And if that is what is best,' he asked, 'what is best for those who have already come to be?'

'Ah, Midas, but this you already know,' said the seilenos. 'The best thing for those who already are is this: *to die soon*.'

Then the seilenos stuck out his tongue, gave a mocking bow, farted, and trotted out of the palace.

*

A few days after this, whilst lost in unsettled and turbulent dreams, Midas was visited by the god Dionysos. The radiant young god leapt into Midas's mind, clad only in the smallest of tunics. 'Midas,' he said. 'Soon I leave for the East, but tonight I have come to thank you.'

The dream-Midas shrank back. 'Thank me? For what do I deserve your thanks, Dionysos?'

The god laughed. 'For the greatest virtue amongst men, that of hospitality. You took in my dear old seilenos. You fed him and entertained him, then you returned him safe to me. I have come to thank you and to grant you a boon.'

'A boon?' Midas remembered the seilenos's words, and he shuddered.

Dionysos laughed. 'Anything you wish, your majesty. The choice is yours.'

Midas thought for a moment, and then he said, 'What I wish for is gold, Dionysos. A king whose touch turned everything to gold would be a fortunate man indeed.'

That was how it all started. When Midas woke the next morning, it was on golden sheets. By his side was his wife. She, too, had turned to gold. His daughter ran in and flung her arms around him, and she became a golden image of herself. His food and table, his servants, the tables and the stools, the pillars of the palace, the bricks and stones, the ground upon which he walked—all turned into the burnished statues.

It had been humiliating to go snivelling back to the god, and to beg—to beg!—for his boon to be reversed. Dionysos laughed as if he had known this is what would happen all along, as if it was nothing more than a wonderful joke. He told Midas to go and wash in the river Paktolos.

So Midas went down to the river, and the river washed him clean of his gift, his curse. Then he returned along the golden road to the golden palace. He passed through the golden gateposts and into the golden feasting hall with its golden dining table and its golden platter on top of which sat a golden pig. He went into the golden bedchamber and saw his golden wife lying on the golden sheets, his golden daughter with her arms open, more beautiful than could be conjured by any sculptor's art. He touched his daughter's cheek, then he drew his hand away.

He walked into the golden gardens where he saw the golden fountain at which, parched, he had bent to drink earlier that day. It was obscene, unspeakable. And as he stood amongst all those riches—the most fortunate and most wretched of men—he knew that every word the seilenos had spoken was true.

In the palace gardens was a tree that had remained wood and fruit and leaf. Hanging from the tree was a single apple. It was not made of gold, but was instead red and green. Midas reached up, plucked the apple, and put it to his mouth. He bit into the skin. The flesh was all juice and fragrance. Then, the juice of the apple running down his chin, the king started to sob.

Later that evening, the king retired to his golden bedchamber and made a vow. 'Henceforth,' he said to himself. 'I will live without gods. Godless I will live and godless I will die. And when I am dead, I will at least be freed from misery.'

King Midas closed his eyes and he slept.

16

Marsyas hitched a passage home from Arkadia on the boat of a deaf fisherman. The fisherman had taken on the satyr because he liked his face, and because he fancied some company. The first two days of the journey were stormy, but the boat was robust and held up well. Marsyas spent most of the time vomiting over the side, but after the storm passed and the sun came out—a pleasant late autumn sun—he stretched out on the deck and relaxed.

It was during the third day of the voyage that he was disturbed by a frenetic fluttering of tiny wings. When he opened his eyes, he saw Hermes hovering above him.

Towards the aft of the boat, his hand on the tiller, the fisherman hardly seemed to notice the fluttering god. He glanced up, and then he shrugged and looked away, setting his eyes on the horizon.

'Marsyas,' Hermes said to the satyr, 'The god Apollo accepts your challenge.'

Marsyas propped himself on his elbow, and grinned at the hovering deity. He felt a sudden warm surge of pride. It felt good. 'The god? Which god?' he said.

'The god Apollo,' Hermes replied. 'Lord of music.'

Marsyas tried to look nonchalant. He made a soft whistling sound through his teeth, and scratched his belly. 'And who might you be?' he asked.

'I am Hermes,' the god said, 'messenger to the gods, patron of thieves, guardian of orators. I have come from the great god Apollo. Apollo has heard your challenge, and he proposes a fair contest, to see who is the greater.'

Hermes descended to hover just a fraction above the wooden boards of the deck. 'The contest will be on Mount Tmolos. Apollo proposes that the contest takes place in the following fashion . . .'

Marsyas gave a dismissive gesture. 'Yes, yes,' he said. 'Whatever the old boy says. Tell him I accept.' Then he pulled out his pipes and put them to his lips, blowing through them so that they made a farting sound.

'You will have to do better than that,' said Hermes.

Marsyas chuckled. 'Maybe I can,' he said, 'and maybe I can't. Now, leave me alone. I've got things to do.' He stretched back out on the deck and closed his eyes.

Hermes was tempted to say something else, but he restrained himself. The satyr's punishment would surely come. The god turned on his winged heels and scudded off over the waves back to Olympos.

The rest of the journey was without incident. They landed on the coast of Asia. Marsyas thanked the fisherman for the passage, and then he followed a little stream inland. He walked for a long time. Night after night the moon waxed and waned and waxed again until at last he could sniff the fragrance of Phrygia on the air. After another day scampering over the hills he could see Mount Tmolos in the distance. He was excited to be almost home, longing to see Kybele again.

They met shortly before sunset. Kybele was walking through the grain fields, exercising her lions, enjoying the cool breezes, and thinking of Dionysos's departure for the East. It was quiet in Phrygia. Many of the seilenoi and satyroi and korybantes had accompanied the god on his journey east, and Kybele felt quite alone. Marsyas's voice—'Halloooo, Kybele! Halloooo!'—gave her a surge of delight.

The goddess looked up to see the satyr hurtling towards her with the aulos in his hand. She stood still and waited for him to reach her.

Grinning and sweating, and for once unmindful of her lions, Marsyas leapt into Kybele's arms. He wriggled and squirmed, covering her cheeks with kisses. 'Marsyas,' she said quietly, 'welcome back.'

The goddess lowered him gently to the ground. The satyr gazed up at her with delight. The afternoon sun was blazing in the western sky. He was home, and everything was perfect.

Kybele pointed to the aulos. 'You found it then, you rascal,' she said, and she reached down to scratch the satyr affectionately behind the ears.

'I got it! I found it!' Marsyas's grin became wider.

Kybele looked at the flute. 'Now all you have to do is learn to play.'

'Learn? But I already know, Kybele. Listen . . .' He squatted down ready to play. Then he faltered. Kybele's smile had gone. Marsyas looked into her eyes, and she held his glance.

'Marsyas,' she said, 'what did I tell you?'

'Kybele?' He affected a look of innocence.

'Marsyas, I told you not to play until you returned to Phrygia.'

Marsyas put the pipes down. 'I only played a *little*,' he said.

'In Arkadia, Marsyas?'

'Just a bit, Kybele, not much.'

The goddess sat down on a boulder and sighed. 'And what if the Olympians had come to hear of your antics?'

Marsyas went very quiet. He hung his head. Kybele reached down and lifted up his chin with her finger. 'Marsyas, *did* the Olympians find out?'

Marsyas winced. 'They didn't mind *very* much,' he said.

'Didn't mind? What did they do, Marsyas?'

Marsyas's lower lip trembled. 'I'm going to have a contest,' he said, as bravely as he could.

'A contest? With whom?'

'With Apollo.'

Kybele's mouth tightened. 'Marsyas,' she said, 'what have you done?'

'It's all right, Kybele. I'm very good. I'll win for certain. I've practised really hard. You should have seen them dancing in Arkadia! If you had seen them dancing in Arkadia, you'd believe me.'

Kybele spoke again. 'Tell me everything, Marsyas. Apollo is a cruel god. He cannot be trusted.'

The goddess took Marsyas in her arms and, hesitatingly at first, the satyr told her what had happened. When he had finished, Kybele shook her head sadly. 'Marsyas,' she said. 'My dear Marsyas! I am so afraid for you.'

Marsyas was irritated by her concern. 'Don't be so gloomy, Kybele. First you should hear me play.'

Kybele smiled. 'Then play, Marsyas,' she said.

So Marsyas clambered from her lap and took up his aulos. He played a few scales in the Phrygian mode. Then he added some ornaments. Next he modulated into another mode—one that does not have a name in any of the treatises of music in the world, so perhaps it should be called the Marsyan mode—and Kybele was so moved that she threw off her tunic so she stood vast and bronze and naked in the setting sun. Then, as Marsyas played, the goddess danced in ecstasy, tears upon her cheeks. She curled her toes in the soft grass. Her heavy belly, breasts, thighs and buttocks swung back and forth. The cool evening breezes dried the sweat on her skin. Eyes half closed in the golden evening light, her hair loose and unpinned, Kybele rocked back and forth with the slow rhythms of her dance.

Marsyas went on playing and Kybele went on dancing until the sun sank over the hills, and the jackals started to call, and both the goddess and the satyr were bathed in moonlight.

Then Marsyas put down his aulos and Kybele's dance came to an end. Without saying anything to the little satyr, Kybele pulled on her robe and clucked her tongue at the lions. The lions got lazily to their feet, and the three of them headed away down the hillside.

Marsyas picked up his pipes and scampered off into the undergrowth to find a place to sleep.

17

Kybele made directly for the palace of Midas. She arrived just as the moon was setting and slipped through the golden palace gates. As she was approaching the bedchamber, she heard the sound of footsteps, delicate and nervy. The goddess ducked behind a golden pillar. It was Hermes, coming out of the palace on his dainty winged feet.

She thought there was something dislikeable about Hermes: she regarded him with something half way between pity and contempt. She waited until the winged god had scuttled his way out of sight. Then she slipped out from behind the pillar into Midas' bedchamber.

The king was sleeping peacefully. Kybele gazed down at him with a tender ache in her heart. Then she spoke. 'Midas,' she said, 'in your dreaming, you have been visited by the god Hermes, who has brought news of a contest. I come to ask you not to trust him.'

Midas turned and let out a deep sigh, but he did not wake. Kybele put her hand on his forehead. It was cool and soothing. 'Midas, my son, I come to ask your assistance.'

The king stirred and groaned.

‘When you come to judge the contest of which Hermes has spoken, Midas, remember your brothers who live in the wilds. Remember your kin. Remember the voices that speak in your thundering blood.’

Then the goddess leaned down and kissed the king on the forehead. In his sleep he sighed with a rare moment of happiness.

‘I will leave now, Midas,’ the goddess said. ‘Farewell.’

For the rest of the night, Midas slept dreamlessly. When he woke the following morning, he felt the previous night’s visitations weighing heavily upon him. He got up, put on his robe, and took a walk in the palace gardens to collect his thoughts. His mind was filled with jumbled and half recollected fragments of dreams. He recalled the god Hermes, a summons to Mount Tmolos, something about a contest in which he was to be a juror. Then—was this the same dream or was it different?—he recalled Kybele laying her hand upon his brow. And from out of the fragments and torn remnants of his dreaming, he could hear the echo of the goddess’s voice: *remember the voices that speak in your thundering blood.*

When have the gods ever spoken clearly? he wondered. When have they not riddled and dissimulated? Midas sighed. Momentarily, he thought of leaving the palace. He would walk into the street, exchange his robes with those of a beggar, cut off his beard and hair, and walk south towards the sun. ‘I will leave,’ he said to himself, ‘and nobody will be able to stop me.’

But the moment he had this thought, he knew that he would not leave. He would remain there in the palace, because he was king, and the kingdom was flourishing. The palace coffers were full. Peasants who lived by the banks of the Paktolos had become rich sifting the soil for gold. The cities were wealthy. The people were happy. They *loved* Midas.

Remember the voices that speak in your thundering blood.

Whatever these dreams and messages mean, Midas said to himself, I must be careful. I must watch my mouth. I will go to Tmolos as the dream has instructed me. And when I have done what I must do, I will return to the palace and hope that thenceforth the gods will leave me alone.

Then Midas walked back into the palace, and sat for a long time, looking at the golden forms of his wife and his daughter.

Remember the voices that speak in your thundering blood, he thought.

18

On the southern slopes of mount Tmolos, it was one of those beautiful, clear autumn days when the air retains a trace, a memory, of the summer that has passed. The sky was almost cloudless, incomparably blue and deep.

Word had got out about the contest between Apollo and Marsyas, and already a vast crowd had gathered. On the hillside, which formed a kind of natural theatre, were thousands of excitable spectators with picnics of bread, wine and cheese. There were men, women, children, minor godlings, goat herding girls, nymphs, scampering satyroi, and lecherous old seilenoi. There were musicians on the hillsides too, playing burlesques of the anticipated contest, one dressed as Apollo with a home-made lyre, another masquerading as Marsyas with a flute made from a reed cut from the riverbed, tootling rival tunes, skipping around each other as they played, wrestling and laughing.

Down below, two benches had been set up for the jurors. Next to the benches was a wooden throne, covered in sheepskins, upon which sat Tmolos, the judge, with his grizzled white hair and beard. He was a god of earlier, slower times, bewildered by the age in which he found himself. He pulled and tugged his beard thoughtfully and hummed tunelessly to himself, waiting for the competition to start.

Seated on the front row of juror's benches were the three mortals on the jury. First there was Midas. He was wearing a golden crown. He wore it not out of pride, but as a reproach, as a reminder of his own foolhardiness. Next to Midas were two timid peasants, looking somewhat overawed, their eyes turned towards the ground. Next there were the Muses, daughters of Zeus and Mnemosyne: Kleio, Euterpe, Thaleia, Melpomene, Terpsikhore, Erato, Polyhymnia, Ourania and Kalliope. On their heads were crowns of feathers, plucked from the arses of the Seirenes. The Muses laughed at the pantomimes being played out in the crowd, pointing and covering their mouths with their hands, letting fly pretty little giggles, sharp as arrowheads. Their voices chimed with the trickling of the streams and with the songs of birds high in the branches. They were beautiful, but nobody in the crowd dared to look at them too directly. The crowd knew how the Muses had blinded Thamyris and Demodokos, how they had turned the daughters of Pierus of Makedonia into a flock of chattering magpies.

Opposite the juror's benches, on the other side of Tmolos's throne, were two stools, one for Apollo and one for Marsyas. Before each stool was a little bronze dish, ready to receive the voting-pebbles of the jury.

Marsyas was the first of the two contestants to arrive. He came in style, riding on Kybele's golden chariot. The lions roared to announce his arrival.

The chariot was followed by a host of satyroi, seilenoi and admirers. The goddess held the lions' reins with a stony-faced resolve. Marsyas, garlanded and exhilarated, clutched his aulos and scampered now to this side now to that as he greeted the audience. There was cheering and applause. Young girls fainted as Marsyas winked at them. Old women lost their composure and cried out, ululated, wept. Others tossed wild flowers at the satyr, calling blessings and good wishes. Marsyas had an enormous hard-on. He was revelling in the attention; but Kybele's face remained as still as marble.

Midas watched them approach. He adjusted the crown upon his head, turning his grey eyes on the goddess and the satyr. He turned away again. He remembered Marsyas as a baby, a mere satyr kid, lying in his cradle, sucking his thumb.

The cart drew to a halt. Marsyas came toppling out onto the grass and lay on his back laughing. Kybele got down with dignity and greeted the aged Tmolos with a smile. The old god replied with a courteous nod of the head. Kybele unhitched her lions from their harnesses and took her seat on the benches reserved for guests-of-honour. The lions curled up together by her feet and closed their eyes. A crowd of inebriated peasants clustered around the prone satyr and lifted him onto their shoulders. They carried him around the field so that the gathered people could hang garlands about his neck. Marsyas was panting with excitement, winking frenetically at the wenches and the goatherd girls and at pretty young boys. A group of satyroi followed behind, improvising songs.

Shortly after the sun passed its zenith, the god Apollo arrived. By this time, a greater part of the audience was drunk. Peasants were dancing in formation. Nymphs were fluttering around making eyes at anyone and everyone. The satyroi were in hot pursuit, waggling their cocks in front of them. The god's coming shattered all this revelry and enthusiasm. The first sign of Apollo's arrival was a cold light that spread across the hillside, dampening the high spirits of the audience. Then there was a sound like a great rush of wind. The revellers and the pipers and the lovers stopped what they were doing and shivered as if it were the heart of winter. Hermes appeared in the far distance, by the peak of Tmolos. He hurtled down the hillside on his winged feet, brandishing his staff, and fluttered to a halt before the crowds. 'The great god Apollo,' he announced.

There was silence: the kind of silence that comes over a wine shop in a dockside town when a known murderer steps through the door; the kind of silence that arises when one thousand different human minds are all united by a single thought: 'If his wrath is to break, may it not be upon me, but upon the shoulders of another.'

Then Apollo appeared. He bore down from the heavens, his helmet glistening. He cut through the air like a fast ship parting the waves of the ocean, and he alighted just before the jury benches. In his right hand, he held his lyre.

The god smiled. He could sense the fear on the hillside. He was pleased with his entrance. The cold light faded, and the god strode towards the stool that had been made ready for him. He seated himself, removed his helmet, and tossed his hair in the afternoon sun. He stretched himself with the vanity of the truly beautiful, showing off the muscles of his spectacular torso. Then he placed the lyre in his lap.

For the first time, Marsyas felt a twinge of fear. He bleated softly.

Then Apollo placed his lyre down and looked at the

crowd, ranged across the hillside. 'Who is my challenger?' he asked.

Marsyas stood up. He looked over at the god, wide-eyed. 'I am,' he said.

19

Marsyas made his way towards the seat next to that of Apollo. Beside the brilliant god, for all the sheen of his satyr-pelt, he looked small and dull.

When the two contestants were seated, Tmolos rose to his feet. He was unsteady on his old legs and the earth shook a little with the effort. Kleio and Euterpe, the Muses, came to his aid. They held his arms and helped lift him into a position where he was more or less upright.

Music? Tmolos thought. He could not see what the fuss was about. Birds sing. Donkeys bray. Cockerels crow. Men and gods chatter, argue, curse, sing. It was all the same to him. All he wanted was for the flowers to grow every spring on the mountain slopes, and for the snows to shroud the peak in whiteness every winter. This was enough entertainment for an arthritic old man who, being immortal, could not even hope for death to relieve him of his burdens.

The ancient god's voice, craggy and broken, had a striking power. 'Ladies and gentlemen of the jury, good people of Phrygia,' he said. 'Welcome.'

He squinted at the crowd. 'Today there will be a contest

in the art of music between a mortal and an immortal, a satyr and a god.'

Apollo frowned.

'Our first contestant is Marsyas, the satyr from Phrygia,' he said.

Tmolos was fond of Marsyas. He had often watched with pleasure as the little satyr played on his slopes. And it was clear that Tmolos was not the only one who liked Marsyas. At the mention of the satyr's name, the crowd erupted into applause, threw flowers, tootled on their home-carved flutes and whistled with their fingers between their teeth. Marsyas was heartened by this show of support. He rose to his feet, lifted his pipes in the air and grinned. Apollo looked on in scorn.

Having taken a standing ovation long enough to pique his rival, Marsyas sat down. The crowd fell silent.

Tmolos continued. 'Facing the Phrygian satyr,' he said, 'is the god Apollo.'

The god of music turned his head to accept the adulation of the crowd, but found it unforthcoming. Nobody cheered. Nobody clapped. There was a terrible silence.

Apollo thought of plagues. He thought of fires from the heavens and of creeping things from the earth. He thought of the gathered celebrants rolling around in agony, their bodies swelling and rupturing with sores. He thought of the sticky sweats that would herald their final days, how the shrine of Asklepios would be overrun with the incurable.

'Let us welcome the god Apollo,' Tmolos prompted.

The people began to clap. Apollo rose to accept the applause.

Tmolos, whose legs were beginning to tremble under the strain of supporting his old body, mumbled, 'Let the contest begin.' Kleio and Euterpe eased him back into his judge's throne. He sank back into the sheepskins with relief.

Apollo spoke next. His voice was cold. 'There must be a stake. There is no contest without a stake.'

Tmolos cocked his head on one side and then he leaned over to consult with his jury. The Muses twittered prettily and Tmolos nodded and listened.

'You are right, Lord Apollo,' Tmolos said. 'There must be a stake. Let us, then, have a stake to be agreed by the two contestants together.'

'Our instruments!' Marsyas cried. 'We stake our instruments!'

It was a big thing, this stake. He did not want to lose his aulos. But he reminded himself that he would not lose, because he already knew that nobody was greater in the art of music.

Apollo shook his head. 'No,' he said, his voice soft and sweet. 'Let us leave the stake open.'

'Open?' asked Marsyas. The ladies and gentlemen of the jury leaned forward with interest.

'What I mean to say,' Apollo said, 'is that the victor chooses all rewards and penalties, and the loser must submit to his choice.'

Marsyas thought. This was better. It would give him the chance to be generous to the defeated god. He would ask Apollo to be his *accompanist* for a final number. He might even give the god a short solo. Then he would send him on his way. This would be reward enough.

'Are you agreed?' Apollo pressed.

Marsyas looked at Apollo and then at the expectant crowd. 'Yes,' Marsyas said. 'I'm agreed.'

'Good,' Apollo said genially. 'Who is to play first?'

Marsyas had no opinion on this. First or second, he was still supreme. He shrugged.

'In that case, I will play second,' Apollo said. 'I look forward to hearing your efforts.' The disdain in his voice was masked by sweetness, but not entirely. Marsyas felt a shiver go through him as Apollo spoke. He shook it off.

Marsyas bunched up his legs and lifted his double pipes. The crowd, suddenly subdued, leaned forward. He put the pipes between his lips. The spectators faded to the fringes of his awareness. He loved playing for an audience, yet when he played it was as if he was alone. He wrapped himself up in music like a protective cape and drove away all thought and fear of harm.

Marsyas started with a single phrase. It was simple and rustic. He knew it would appeal to the audience, which was also simple and rustic. The final note of the phrase lingered, sweet and gentle in the morning sun.

Now Marsyas played the same phrase again, an echo. He played it a third time, but this time he changed it just a little, bending the notes so that it gave the audience a delicious shiver of sorrow. Stillness descended over the mountainside. The gods of the winds, of the gusts, of the minor flurries became silent and listened. The leaves on the trees hung motionless in the still air. No creatures moved through the grass, not even the smallest insect. Apollo held his breath, his face grim. Midas the king smiled to himself. A glimmer of perplexity passed over the Muses' faces, as if they could not quite understand Marsyas's music.

Then Marsyas took a deep breath, and played a staggering series of arpeggios that made the audience shout with joy. They began to rise to their feet as Marsyas played on. '*Ai!*' they shouted. '*Hai! Oi! Ai!*'

Even old Tmolos seemed affected by this music. He bobbed his head from side to side. The notes came in bursts and flurries. Marsyas played with his eyes closed, tapping his foot, his cheeks puffed out like fat purple plums.

Apollo beckoned to Hermes. The little messenger god fluttered over and whispered in his ear. 'Apollo!' he said. 'What are we to do?'

'We must wait,' Apollo whispered. His lips curled in distaste. The satyr was far better than he had anticipated.

'Apollo, what if he *wins*?'

Apollo did not reply, but his face darkened. He watched as Marsyas played a final, shimmering cadenza. The crowd roared their approval.

Then Marsyas played a final note—so high that it was almost out of the range of hearing. He held it for a long time.

A hush came over the mountainside as the final note faded towards silence.

Somebody in the crowd began to clap, then a second, a third, ten, one hundred, ten thousand spectators cheering and clapping. The audience surged forward. The crowd mobbed Marsyas, jostling the god Apollo in their enthusiasm. They lifted the satyr—brave challenger of the gods, plucky under-goat—high upon their shoulders, and he held up his pipes, grinning in triumph.

Tmolos gestured to the Muses, and they helped him struggle to his feet. His cleared his throat. The rumbling sound echoed across the valley, calling the excitable crowd to order. 'Order!' he said. 'This is a court of judgement. Return to your seats, please. Allow me to invite our second contestant, the god Apollo, to play.'

The crowd reassembled itself into something like good order.

Marsyas returned, grinning wildly, to the stool next to Apollo. The god picked up his lyre, played an arpeggio to check the tuning.

'Good luck, brother,' said Marsyas.

The god Apollo gave the satyr a sour look. Then he closed his eyes and started to play.

20

The moment Apollo plucked his first notes, the mood on the hillside changed. The listeners became subdued, cowed, as if the crystalline sounds that came from Apollo's lyre—a music of measure and order, hard and exquisite—planted a silent terror in their hearts. This was a music in which everything had its place, in which not a single note was wasted. It was cold, precise and perfect.

The spectators were too terrified to shuffle or to shift. They listened in perfect stillness. Apollo's face was expressionless as he played. His fingers moved with the utmost exactitude. It was music without any imperfections, and it made those who listened to it out on the hillside feel small and dull and unimportant. If Marsyas's music had filled their hearts, it was as if the music of Apollo was tearing their hearts to tatters. And yet this music was indescribably, unspeakably beautiful.

Apollo closed his performance quietly, without any of the drama of Marsyas's cadenza. The final few phrases reprised the whole perfectly. The last note lingered and died. The silence it left behind was heavy with fear and wonder. Apollo lifted his fingers from the cow-gut strings of the lyre and opened his eyes. A shudder went through the crowd. Nobody applauded. A faint, sweet perspiration was visible on Apollo's brow.

Tmolos's head was bowed. He sat like this for a long time, then he raised his eyes to the contestants and looked at each in turn. After this, he turned to face the jury. 'Now our two contestants have played, I must ask the jury to cast their votes for the verdict.'

Marsyas frowned. This was not what he expected. As Apollo played, it had felt as if the competition had somehow changed terms. The spectators, too, were puzzled, uneasy. To ask which was better, the music of Marsyas or the arpeggiated sublimities of Apollo, was like asking which was better, a skinful of wine or a constellation of stars. It was like asking whether one should prefer a piece of cheese or a mouse. It was like trying to divine whether tumbling stream is greater than a volcano. The satyr flexed his toes.

Tmolos nodded to the jurors. They rose in turn and went to offer their pebbles. First it was the turn of the Muses. Kleio, mother of Hyakinthos, placed her pebble in Marsyas's dish. There was a round of applause. Marsyas grinned. Euterpe was next. She walked over to Apollo and placed a pebble in the dish that was set before the god. The smile disappeared from Marsyas's face. After Euterpe came Thaleia. Her vote, at least, was inevitable. Thaleia and Apollo had fucked in the past, giving birth to the korybantes. There had never been a bond of love between them, but it was Apollo who had spent a night between her thighs and not Marsyas.

Erato, too, favoured the Olympian god. Marsyas shifted on his seat. For the first time, it occurred to him that he might lose. He closed his eyes. He wanted to be close to Kybele, to nuzzle at her milk-filled breasts, to have her scratching him behind his ears. He wanted the whole thing over with. As for Melpomene and Terpsikhore, they went the same way as Thaleia and Erato.

But then Polyhymnia rose, her red tresses blazing. She took her pebble, went over to stand before Apollo, smiled sweetly, and tossed the pebble to one side into Marsyas's dish. The satyr was startled. He looked up at Polyhymnia. She glanced down at him and puckered her lovely lips into the slightest trace of a kiss. Kalliope was next, sweetest and fairest by temperament of all the Muses. She followed Polyhymnia's lead. Then came Ourania. She chose Apollo.

There were now three pebbles in Marsyas's plate and six in Apollo's: a fair lead for the god, but the mortals were still to vote.

The first of the peasants walked up to the two contestants. He looked Apollo in the eye. Apollo could read the meaning of his look. *I know that you may choose to strike me down*, it meant. *I know that you have the power to kill my whole family by plague. But I will vote how I choose.*

The peasant put his pebble in Marsyas's plate.

Marsyas looked into the two dishes. He was not very good at counting. It was not that he did not have the mental acuity, only that he got bored, usually somewhere around the count of two or three. By the count of four his mind was usually so far away that he had to begin once again. He frowned and peered into his bowl: a lot of pebbles. He looked into Apollo's bowl: also a lot of pebbles. He began to count off the pebbles in his bowl on his fingers, but each time he started, he got lost after three and started again from scratch.

Whilst Marsyas was wrestling with these difficult calculations, the second of the two peasants, a more timorous man, rose. He placed his pebble where his fellow countryman's had been. He did not glance at the god, or the satyr, or the audience. He placed his pebble apologetically, as if he hoped that nobody might notice.

Finally it was the turn of the king, Midas. He stood with dignity and walked over to the two contestants. Midas bowed towards Apollo.

Remember the voices that speak in your thundering blood, he thought.

'My choice is with your opponent, Sir,' he said to Apollo. 'Your music, although beautiful, chills me.'

The king placed his pebble in Marsyas's plate.

Tmolos counted the votes, making sure that he added up the number of pebbles carefully, so that there could be no mistake. He performed this operation three times over. Then the ancient god of the mountains turned to the audience.

'The contest,' he said, 'is a draw.'

21

A rumble of displeasure went through the crowd. A draw? Was it possible? What was the point of a contest if it ended in a draw? They wanted a victor and a loser. They wanted one player exalted and the other humiliated. And if they would have preferred Marsyas as victor and Apollo as loser, they would have settled for the reverse. At least, had Apollo won, they could have contented themselves with grumbling.

Apollo gazed at king Midas with cold hatred. Dark thoughts passed through the god's mind. The bastard king, spawn of a drunken goat and a slattern goddess, was going to fucking suffer. He was going to be fucking sorry. But first it was necessary to resolve the problem of this humiliating and undignified draw. Who had been fucking stupid enough to have twelve on the jury, instead of eleven or thirteen? As for the two peasants: they too would be sorry.

Tmolos scratched his head. He had not anticipated this outcome. The Muses talked amongst themselves, justifying their choices to each other, arguing sweetly.

Then, somewhere out in the crowd, a woman in middle age stood up. She had the serious bearing, the fearlessness, that comes from having suffered through childbirth and grieving more than any man can imagine. 'We all know that Marsyas was better,' she yelled. 'Give the prize to Marsyas. Tmolos, yours is the casting vote. We who have lived our lives on your slopes beg you to vote for the satyr.'

She sat down again. Her voice was echoed from elsewhere in the crowd. 'Give the prize to Marsyas!'

'The satyr! Long live the satyr!'

Apollo's face twitched. Hermes fluttered over and cupped his hand to the god's ear. Apollo smiled, and Hermes flitted over to Tmolos and whispered to him also. Tmolos nodded gravely, then he held up his hand to still the crowd.

'It is not the place for a judge to arbitrate,' he said. 'And thus we will have a retrial. Any contest must only have a single winner and a single loser. It is necessary, in the end, to pass judgement. So I would ask both contestants to play a second time.'

'No retrial!' the woman shouted back. 'Give the prize to Marsyas!'

Tmolos continued. 'At the suggestion of the god Hermes, I propose the following modification. Let the contestants play their instrument upside down. Other than that, everything will happen as before: Marsyas will play first, followed by Apollo. The voting will take place in the same fashion as before.'

Marsyas picked up his aulos. This time he would play better, and there would be no uncertainty about the result. The crowd was on his side.

Tmolos hushed the crowd with a wave of his hand. Then he looked gravely at the jury. 'Ladies and gentlemen of the jury, I ask you to listen carefully and to make your judgements wisely.'

Midas looked deep in thought and stroked at the end of his beard. The two peasants shuffled with embarrassment, afraid to look at the Muses or at Apollo.

Marsyas hopped off his stool. The challenge was an easy one. *Let the contestants play their instrument upside down*. He would have no trouble with this. He was no stranger to acrobatics. So Marsyas waved at the crowd, and then he turned himself arse-over-toe to balance upon his head. His horns anchored him firmly in the soft soil. It felt good to have the wind in his nether parts. His cock became hard.

Then, his backside pointed towards the heavens and his head towards the earth, the satyr put his pipes to his lips.

Apollo motioned to Tmolos and sent Hermes scudding over on his gossamer ankle-wings to speak with the old judge.

Tmolos nodded his head. 'Marsyas,' he said, 'you have misunderstood. The stipulation is that the *instrument* should be upside down, not the *player*.'

Marsyas scowled. With a hop, he tipped himself upright again. 'The pipes?' he asked. 'You want the *pipes* to be upside down, but *me* to be the right way up?'

Tmolos nodded.

Marsyas was disappointed. It would have been funny to see Apollo with his arse in the air. He returned to his stool and looked at his pipes carefully. He could see a trace of a smile on Apollo's lips.

Marsyas had never tried playing the pipes the other way round. There had been no need. He always blew into the same end and this seemed to serve him well. But a pipe is a pipe: a hollow tube for air to rush through and to sing sweetly. What did it matter which direction the air went?

Marsyas put the double pipes in his mouth. He calibrated

his fingers along the length of the reeds. Should he play the same tune, he wondered, or a different one? Or should he start the same and then modulate into something altogether surprising? That would send them wild. The crowd would like that—and, perhaps, the jury too.

He breathed in and filled his lungs. His diaphragm expanded, cool air rushed in through his flaring nostrils. Slowly, he let the air out.

There was a hissing sound, like a summer wind passing through trees and reed beds. It was a murmur, a sigh, an exhalation. But it was not music.

Marsyas frowned. This was strange. If you blew one way there was music; but if you blew another way there was none. Perhaps, he thought, the music wasn't *ready* to come. He removed the pipes from his mouth and waited a few moments. Then he returned the pipes to his lips and blew again.

The same thing. A rushing of air and nothing else. Marsyas furrowed his brow in concentration and blew harder. His cheeks bulged outwards like two plums. But the music still refused to come.

The satyr removed the pipes from his mouth and laid them across his lap. This had never happened before. He was worried, but not too worried. Perhaps tracking tunes was like tracking nymphs: sometimes, on a first or second attempt, they slipped out of your grasp; but on the third attempt, success was certain. Music could not simply be *played*; it had to be *seduced*, drawn out of its secret hiding places with gentleness and patience.

Marsyas scratched his balls trying to look unconcerned. Then he squinted up at the sun. When he felt ready, he picked up the pipes again, put them to his mouth, and played.

Again nothing. Just a rushing of air: *Pffffssst*.

He blew harder. A vein bulged and pulsed on his forehead.

Still nothing.

His shoulders arched with tension. *This can't be right!* Marsyas thought.

The members of the jury seemed confused, as if they were wondering how a musician who had recently been so skilled had suddenly become so inept.

Marsyas redoubled his efforts. His face turned purple, his eyes bulged like the eyes of a lunatic drooling at the shrine of a god of healing. His nostrils flared. His ears were pinned back with the effort of playing. But there was no music.

Desperately, he gave a final puff with all his strength. The only sound that emerged was a barrage of farts.

Pap-pap-pap-pap-pax!

'Stop, Marsyas! What are you doing?' somebody in the audience called out.

Pap-pap-pap-pap-pax!

'Marsyas, what has happened to you?' called another.

Pap-pap-pap-pap-pax!

'Marsyas, where has your talent gone?' shouted a third.

Pap-pap-pap-pap-pax!
Pap-pap-pap-pap-pax!
Pap-pap-pap-pap-pax!

Then, seeing that it was useless, Marsyas rose to his feet. His face was now red with anger. Like Athene before him, he hurled down the aulos. Then the satyr turned to Apollo. 'You knew this would happen!' he bleated. 'You knew!'

'*Order! Order!*' It was Tmolos. The mountain god was fond of Marsyas, and he had no liking for the Olympian; but the court had rules, and rules should be followed to the end. 'Be seated, so that your opponent may play.'

Marsyas sat down and drew up his legs. He rested his forehead on his furry knees.

On the hillside, a whispering of unease passed through the crowd.

The satyr's shoulders shook with silent sobs as Apollo picked up his lyre.

22

The god turned his lyre hornside-down and rested it in his lap. It was not particularly comfortable, but it was playable. He closed his eyes, put his fingers to the strings, and started to play.

And who would not be staggered by his sheer artistry? For the music Apollo played was doubly inverted, once by the turning of his lyre upside-down and a second time by the skill of his playing. For it was the same music as before, but the music itself was turned on its head, so that the pitch fell where before it had risen, and it rose where before it had fallen. Apollo's music was crystalline and jewel-like. Its coldness and rigour made Marsyas tremble.

When the god finished playing, the crowd did not clap. They were too overawed, too terrified. The god put down his lyre and bowed his head.

Everybody knew what the verdict would be. But due process had to be followed. Tmolos indicated to the jury. Each of them in turn rose in silence, bearing their pebbles with them to lay in front of the contestants. Kleio, Euterpe and Thaleia placed their pebbles in Apollo's dish. They could not do otherwise.

Erato, Melpomene and Terpsikhore all voted as they had before. When Polyhymnia came to cast her vote, the satyr looked up at her in hope. She walked with head held down, not meeting Marsyas's eyes. She dropped the pebble in Apollo's dish and sighed, as if to suggest that her vote, born out of her sense of justice, was nevertheless cast against her will. Ourania and Kalliope followed in Polyhymnia's tracks.

The peasants voted next, both in favour of the god. Eleven votes were cast, and the dish before Marsyas was quite empty.

The last vote belonged to Midas. The king rose, adjusted the golden crown, and walked towards the two musicians. There could be only one choice. Marsyas had not played a single note. How could Midas not offer his pebble to the Olympian?

But as he went to cast his vote, the king's legs became unsteady. A pulsing sound throbbed in his ears. He shook his head. The pebble in his hand was cold and damp. He reached out to place the pebble before Apollo. His hand shook as he extended his arm.

Then the voice returned to him. *Remember the voices that speak in your thundering blood.*

As iron is tugged at by a magnet, Midas's hand moved over the empty plate that was set in front of Marsyas. The king's fingers opened and the pebble dropped with a clatter into the bowl of hammered bronze.

Immediately Midas wished to retract, to recall the pebble, to say that he had miscast his vote. But there is no going back on vote that is already cast. The king turned away and walked back to his seat, shoulders hunched.

Tmolos readied himself to pronounce the verdict. Kleio and

Euterpe helped him stand. Marsyas, although not good at counting, was aware of how badly things had gone.

'To the satyr Marsyas is given a single vote,' announced Tmolos. 'And to the god Apollo are given the remainder, to the number of eleven.'

The mountain god paused and looked at both of the contestants in turn. 'Therefore,' he said, 'it is my duty as judge to proclaim the god the winner of this contest.'

A murmur of polite applause rippled across the field. Marsyas was hunched and sobbing. Apollo turned to the satyr and tapped him on the shoulder. Marsyas looked up. 'Your instrument,' Apollo said. His voice had no trace of kindness.

Marsyas looked up, his eyes red with weeping. He handed over the aulos. Apollo took the pipes and broke them over his knee. Then he knelt down and gently lifted Marsyas's head, taking the satyr's chin between his fingers. He stroked Marsyas's beard and gazed into his oblong pupils. He was so close that Marsyas could smell the rancid ambrosia on his breath. 'You have over-reached yourself, my friend,' Apollo murmured.

Marsyas tried to turn his head away, but Apollo tugged sharply at the satyr's beard, so they were eye to eye. 'Now,' Apollo went on, almost in a whisper, 'what shall I ask for my prize?'

Marsyas trembled a little.

Apollo studied Marsyas's face. 'If you had a cape, for example, I would ask you for that. Or a tunic of woven linen, perhaps. You see, it will soon be winter, and I fear the cold. Perhaps you have something you could give me, even if it is very rough and simple.'

Marsyas shook his head.

'No cape?'

The satyr shook his head again.

'Well,' said Apollo, 'I am feeling generous, so I will ask you for something small, something unimportant. Would you be willing to give me something small and unimportant, Marsyas?'

Marsyas nodded, sniffing back the tears.

Apollo smiled at the satyr. The little creature, poor and miserable thing that he was, attempted a smile back.

'This gift,' Apollo said, 'is so very small, Marsyas, that it is hardly worth mentioning.'

'Anything, Apollo,' Marsyas bleated.

Apollo paused. Then he leaned in and whispered, 'What I want, my friend, is your *skin*.'

PART IV
SKIN

23

When Tmolos stood to announce Apollo's chosen prize, a shudder passed over the hillside, as if the sun had momentarily passed behind the cloud. For a moment, everything was still. Nobody dared move. Apollo was smiling a small, satisfied smile.

Kybele came over to Marsyas and put her arms around him in an attempt to soothe him. She ran her fingers through his fur. She could feel him trembling with horror and dread and terror. What one god has done, another may not undo. Marsyas was beyond all helping. What was going to happen was unthinkable; what was going to happen would happen anyway.

The old mountain god, seeing that his job was finished, looked round. His eyes were glazed with weariness. 'Court dismissed,' he said. Then he turned his back on the crowd and with faltering steps made his way back up to his peak. The members of the jury all rose. The Muses tripped off across the fields, holding hands and laughing in the evening sunshine. The two peasant jurors disappeared into the crowd, ashamed of the part that they had played in this most terrible of judgements. Both would be found dead a week later, at the foot of the rocky cliffs of mount Tmolos. Midas wrapped his robe about him, and started on his way back to the palace, deep in thought.

Apollo went over to where Kybele was holding Marsyas. 'Leave him, Kybele,' he said. And—because she would have to leave Marsyas to his fate sooner or later, because she could not prevent what was going to happen from happening—the goddess did as she was asked.

The god picked out several peasants from the crowd and issued them with instructions. The peasants trussed and tied the shuddering Marsyas until he was bound firmly. Then Apollo instructed them to watch over him, and to ensure that he did not escape. 'I have some small business to attend to,' he said. 'I will be back soon.'

Then Apollo was gone. The peasants were left guarding Marsyas the satyr, who was starting to let out little bleats of dread.

As Midas was heading back to the palace, taking the quiet mountain paths where he would not risk meeting anyone, the god of music, Apollo, appeared before him in an effulgence of light. When the king saw the god, a terrible weariness descended over him. Since his vow to have no more to do with gods, the gods had taken more interest in him than ever. 'Apollo,' said Midas, 'why detain me further? Let an old man return home to rest.'

Apollo's face was stern. 'Tell me, Midas,' he said, 'why did you cast your vote against me?'

'It is the privilege of the jury to vote as they see fit,' Midas said. 'Now, please, allow me to pass.'

'And the second time?' Apollo asked. 'You cast your vote

against me a second time, preferring no music to the music that I played?'

'I did.'

'And that, too, is your privilege as a juror?'

'It is, yes,' Midas replied.

'You are clearly no lover of beauty.'

'I am an old man. I have no use for beauty.'

'And you are a fool.'

'I can do nothing other than vote according to the dictates of my heart.'

Apollo laughed. 'And was it your heart you followed when you asked Dionysos for the gift of gold? Perhaps your heart is not your friend, Midas.'

Midas did not reply.

'Your heart makes a fool of you, Midas. It needs reining in. A man with a raging heart is like a wild bull in a potter's shop. Everything becomes broken.'

'It makes no difference, Lord Apollo,' Midas said. 'You were victorious and have no complaint against me. Please, let me pass.'

'No difference?' Apollo asked. 'Then maybe this will make no difference either.' Then the god grasped Midas by the beard and wrestled him to the ground. The king's golden crown tumbled from his head. Apollo drove a knee hard into the king's chest. He felt Midas slacken beneath him, and then he reached up to finger the old man's left ear. 'You dumb fuck, Midas,' he said. 'You have the ears of a man, but you do not use them. It seems that you are no better than an ass.'

Midas felt a strange tearing sensation to either side of his head. Then Apollo blazed with light and was gone. Midas staggered to his feet. Suddenly, the world had become loud.

His head thundered with sounds made large, harsh, different. Midas clutched at the sides of his head, and where there had once been simple folds of flesh he felt great protuberances. He staggered over to the side of the road where there was a pool of still water and he gazed down. He saw his old, lined face and, to either side, the tall ears of an ass, brown and flecked with the white of old age. The veins glowed red where the evening sun shone through.

Midas took off his royal sash and wound it around his head as a turban, making sure that the ears were tucked inside out of sight. The fabric muffled the thundering of the world.

He started on his way back to the palace.

24

Marsyas lay on the ground, his feet bound at the ankles and his hands tied behind his back. He was hunched into a ball, shivering.

When he returned from his business with Midas, Apollo dismissed the peasant guard. He crouched down and stroked Marsyas's pelt, speaking to him as one would to a distressed child. Marsyas flinched from the god's touch.

Hermes stood with his hand on his hip, supervising a reluctant group of shepherds and satyroi who were making ready with the implements of torture. One, a local blacksmith, sharpened a knife on a stone, drawing it back and forth. The rasp of metal against rock sent ripples through Marsyas's flesh. A couple of satyroi carried dishes to catch the dribbling fluids. Some way off, the place of torture was being prepared. A group of peasants had cleared an area beneath a pine tree of scrub and detritus. Now they were tending a fire, so that the ground could be scorched, because a place of slaughter must always be set apart, empty of life. The flames crackled as they swallowed up pine needles. The peasants stood in a circle, making sure the fire did not spread.

Kybele had gone. Unable to bear the spectacle, she had taken herself away to a grove nearby, where she sat, her head covered with her shawl, and sobbed great heaving sobs. Never had her heart felt heavier.

On the killing ground, the flames died down. The peasants doused the embers with water. The smoke came up in great plumes, hung over the mountainside, making the sun's evening rays weak, and then dispersed.

When the execution place was ready, Apollo ordered the peasants to drag Marsyas into the scorched arena. The satyr cried out for a mouthful of wine so that the coming agonies might be eased. The satyroi holding the dishes pleaded with the god to allow this small concession. Apollo refused. 'This is not a drinking party,' he said. 'This is about justice. And justice curdles when mixed with wine.'

Marsyas begged and whined until Apollo grasped him by the neck, pushing him up against the trunk of the pine tree. 'You want a slow flaying or a quick flaying, you piece of goat shit?' he asked. 'Because the more you whinge, the slower it will be.' Then he spat, just once, in the satyr's face.

Marsyas whimpered and Apollo let him drop. As he slumped to the ground, the bark of the pine tree scraped the skin of his back. It was sore.

Marsyas lay silently on the scorched earth, paralysed by something worse than dread. Apollo tied a rope to his bound ankles and tossed the other end over the branch. He noticed how the lower branches had been singed by the fire. The satyroi stood at the ready with their dishes. Hermes looked on, a smile playing around his mouth. Apollo hauled on the rope until Marsyas was suspended. The satyr's arms dangled, his wrists dragging in the charcoal dust.

Apollo nodded to Hermes, and the lord of herds, who was skilled in the arts of butchery, smiled. Hermes was looking forward to this. He took the knife from the blacksmith, and as he did so, his hand trembled with excitement. He was skilled in the flaying of all kinds of carcasses, but he had never done a satyr before, nor anything living.

Apollo crouched down so that he was eye-to-eye with the upended Marsyas. He kissed him on the lips. Then, unexpectedly, he laughed. Marsyas moved his lips. '*What*?'

The god looked at him affectionately. 'Standing on your head a second time, Marsyas?' he laughed. 'Twice in a single day?'

Marsyas did not reply. Apollo gave the satyr a nudge and he rotated slowly at the end of the rope. Then Apollo took a step backwards. 'Let's get started,' he said. 'He's yours, Hermes.'

Apollo seated himself and prepared to play. As Hermes advanced towards the satyr, Apollo's hands hovered above the strings of the lyre. Then he started to play, and it seemed to Marsyas, hanging upside down from the pine tree, that the music itself was an ordeal, an agony that prefigured the greater agony of the knife.

Autumn is not a good time for flaying. In the winter the skin is good, the leather and the hair strong and of excellent quality; but autumn the skin is weak and difficult to cure. Hermes fluttered over and circled round Marsyas a few times, wondering where to make the first cut. The satyr was almost motionless, except for his trembling lip, and his eyes, which tried to follow the flitting god.

Then with the speed and agility of one practised in his art, Hermes cut circles around the skin by Marsyas's ankles and wrists. In a goat, these would be where the skin ended in the hardness of hooves, and Hermes did not want to waste time dealing with hands and feet. Then the god slipped the tip of the knife into the skin just above the satyr's cock, and he sliced downwards, opening his skin from the lower belly all the way to the top of the breastbone.

Marsyas let out a choked cry. It was lost somewhere in his throat, drowned out by Apollo's music. His body jerked and convulsed as Hermes went about his work. He spewed a watery vomit that filled his nose with bitterness and dripped downwards onto the burned soil. Hermes fluttered back with distaste.

Then Hermes made another couple of swift cuts from the breastbone down to the wrist joints, and two more from Marsyas's groin up to the ankles. He carefully sliced the skin at the base of the neck, using light cuts—the sign of an expert butcher. Marsyas bleated in pain and his body juddered. The god found all this jerking and shuddering irritating. It made his job more difficult, less elegant. When the knife cut through the muscle, it drew blood, and one of the satyroi had to run with a dish to catch it as it flowed down to the ground, thick and red.

Marsyas's eyes were starting to glaze over. His breast was rising and falling in desperate gasps. Hermes put down the knife on the scorched ground. The cuts had all been made to his satisfaction. He started to prise open the skin of Marsyas's torso. Apollo played on, eyes closed.

Hermes peeled Marsyas as one would a slack-skinned fruit, ripe and ready for the eating. He prised apart the skin of his torso, then he used the weight of his body to pull downwards, stripping the skin from ankles to head.

Marsyas was naked: nerves exposed, veins pulsing, organs

throbbing in evidence of his still continuing life. The heaving chambers of his lungs swelling beneath his rib-cage with his erratic breath. His skin, cut from his body, was almost clean, smirched with a little blood and stray flesh where the knife had gone in too deep.

Marsyas drifted out of consciousness, but unconsciousness was not oblivion. The darkness into which he fell was made of pain, woven from Apollo's terrible music.

Hermes felt as if it was all rather disappointing, something of an anti-climax. He let the knife fall, and he gestured to the huddle of satyroi. They scurried over and untied the rope, carefully lowering Marsyas down to the ground.

The first flies started to appear, buzzing around the newly stripped carcass, feasting on Marsyas's living juices. Hermes passed the skin to one of the satyroi. 'Wash it,' he said.

Apollo's music came to a close. He put down the lyre and his eyes slid over to where Marsyas was lying unconscious. He looked upon the satyr without great interest. The contest was over and he had exacted his prize. Now the whole business bored him.

'Shall I break his skull?' Hermes asked.

'Why?' Apollo was surprised.

'To tan the hide with the brains,' Hermes said, 'as one would with a goat or a cow.'

Apollo shook his head. 'No,' he said. He did not care about the hide. All he wanted was for Marsyas's agony to be prolonged. 'Leave him,' Apollo said. 'I am sick of mortals. Let us go.'

The sky was now dark, and in the darkness it was possible to see fires lit on the hillsides. Nymphs and satyroi, farmers and cowherds were huddling together, keeping vigil until Marsyas breathed his last. Apollo looked at them with distaste. There was something repulsive about them. And, to tell the truth, he was disappointed. He had imagined the flaying as a great victory, surrounded by cheering and celebration. But it had not felt like that. He hated mortals, but he longed for their love. And however much he told himself that their love should not matter, that he was a god and they were the scum of the earth, somehow it always *did* matter. It mattered in the way it mattered when the nymphs he hunted down and fucked lay as limp as corpses whilst he moved on top of them. *Why didn't they love him?* he thought.

Apollo turned his gaze to the satyroi who had attended to this atrocity. They were weeping. The one who had gone to wash the hide returned and threw it on the ground.

I will have some celebration, Apollo said to himself. *The occasion must be marked with some celebration.*

'Get up, you little fuckers,' the god said. 'And if you do not want to end up like Marsyas you better do as I tell you. How about singing me a nice farewell song?'

'A song?' The teeth of the satyroi chattered in fear.

'A goat song.'

One of the braver satyroi tried to protest. 'Lord Apollo, please . . . we don't feel like singing.'

Apollo looked at Hermes. 'Take this one,' he said, 'and skin him too. Hang him from the rope from which Marsyas was hung.'

This was enough to change their minds. The satyroi clustered around Apollo, pleading and promising. 'We're sorry, Lord Apollo! Forgive us! We'll do anything you ask! Anything!

We'll do you the best song you have ever heard! What kind of song do you want?'

Apollo smiled, and he felt a surge of affection for the satyroi. They were charming creatures, really. 'I want a victory song,' the god said. 'And make it a good one. If I do not like it, I will skin the lot of you. Understood?'

The satyroi grinned and bobbed their heads obsequiously. Then they started to sing.

The satyr called Marsyas
had an overweening pride,
but Apollo beat him hollow
and he stripped him of his hide.

He had thought to storm Olympos
with the beauty of his playing,
but Apollo beat him hollow,
and he punished him with flaying.

We were rooting, we admit,
for our brother and our friend:
but Apollo beat him hollow—
what a nasty, sticky end!

In the sight of judge and jury,
it was absolutely fair,
so Apollo beat him hollow,
and he stripped Marsyas bare.

As they sang, the fragrance of the night flowers began to fill the mountainside. Overhead stretched the Milky Way, that great river of stars. The two gods, Hermes and Apollo, took their leave of this world of mortals, Apollo carrying the flayed skin of the satyr and Hermes going ahead of him. The satyroi continued to sing until the moon was high.

So Apollo, Lord Apollo—
though it's rather hard to swallow—
you're a tricky act to follow,
you outclassed that satyr's din:

You're a pretty splendid fellow
with your melodies so mellow:
are you happy with my song now?
Will you let me keep my skin?

Are you happy with my song now?
Will you let me keep my skin?

25

Semi-conscious on account of the pain, the satyr lay dripping his life-blood into the earth. The hillsides were almost silent. Far off in the distance, up on Olympos, Apollo picked up his lyre. He was restless, his head thumping with a kind of thunder. He played to soothe his agitation.

Kybele returned to the place where the satyr's body lay. She took off her upper tunic and lay it on the ground. A group of satyroi clustered around the goddess, hiding in her skirts, whimpering slightly, peeping at Marsyas, slicked with his own juices. They reached out and touched each other for reassurance, as if to say, 'Do not worry, brother! Your own skin still sits snug upon your flesh!'

Kybele put her arms around the flayed Marsyas and lifted the quivering bundle. She laid it gently down on her tunic. Marsyas's lips moved, feverish with pain, but no words came. Kybele turned to a little satyr who was cowering by her side. 'Little friend,' she murmured, 'call Hekate.'

'But, Kybele,' said the little satyr, 'where will I find her?'

'Go to a crossroads and call,' Kybele said. 'Tell her that Kybele wishes to speak with her.'

The satyr scuttled off over the hillside, making for the nearest crossroads.

Not long after, nymphs arrived from their hiding places, and started to lament. 'O Marsyas,' they sang, 'most wretched of all living beings, swinging from a shaggy pine, you strove against Apollo and lost! No more through the pine-clad hills of Phrygia will you play your melodies or utter your sweet notes . . .'

Kybele silenced them, irritated by their mournful songs. 'Be quiet,' she said. 'Marsyas lives. Lamentations are for the dead.'

And it was true: Marsyas was still alive. His lips were moving, his body trembling. Kybele leaned down and reached out to touch him, but then withdrew her hand. Marsyas's lips spasmed. 'I want to die,' he said, his voice almost inaudible.

'No,' said Kybele. 'You will live, Marsyas. I will make sure you live.'

'Let me die,' Marsyas whispered.

'Then I will be alone, Marsyas. You cannot die. I will see that you live.'

'Please, Kybele.'

'No,' the goddess said. Then she started to weep. And when they saw the goddess weeping in the moonlight, the satyrs and nymphs began to weep also. Their tears fell to the ground and became a trickle. The trickle swelled to a stream. The stream ran downhill, gathering the tears of all who were grieving—peasants, nymphs, seilenoi, satyroi—and it became a river that cut a swathe through the earth and swept west towards the sea. And as the river opened into the sea, the sea became more salt than it had ever been before.

They called the river Marsyas, in honour of the satyr.

26

Hekate appeared out of the obscurity of the gathering night, muttering and spitting. By her side was the trembling satyr who had been sent to fetch her. The old goddess shuffled along, her spine bent, a blazing torch in her right hand. The little satyr guided her to Kybele's side. The younger goddess rose to meet her. 'Welcome, Hekate! You look angry. What troubles you?'

Hekate spat a gobbet of spit. It fell into the grass with a hiss. 'You call an old woman from her rest? And for what?'

The old crone tottered a little, and Kybele reached out an arm to steady her. In the torchlight, Kybele could see the milky cataracts over Hekate's left eye. The other eye was dim. The old goddess sniffed at the air. 'Tell me who you are. By your smell you are some kind of god.'

'I am Kybele,' the goddess said.

'Kybele, eh? Why have you bothered me? I am old and tired. Was it you who sent some satyr to the crossroads to yell for me?'

'It was, Hekate.'

Hekate looked round to see if there was anyone who could

relieve her of her torch. She saw a satyr sitting doing nothing and made a *tsk! tsk!* sound through her teeth, the kind of sound that only the old know how to make. The satyr understood and took her torch.

Kybele grasped Hekate's old hands. Then she knelt down in the moonlight before the venerable goddess. 'Hekate, goddess of old things, guardian of forgotten wisdom, my friend lies dying.'

'Death!' Hekate muttered. 'Well, he is lucky. You think I do not long for death?' She tried to pull her hands away, but Kybele held firm. 'You are a goddess, Kybele. You should know that death is a great gift. The alternatives are old age and boredom. Why should I deny anyone death?'

'I do not ask that you deny death,' Kybele said. 'Only that you forestall it. My friend is Marsyas, a satyr.'

'Is it his carcass I can smell?' Hekate asked. She sucked at the inside of her cheeks with her toothless gums. 'He smells ready for the roasting.'

'He has met great misfortune.'

'I know this satyr,' she said. 'I know him by his smell. He stole offerings of mine in Arkadia. Why should I help him?'

'Because I love him,' Kybele said.

'Kybele, let your friend die and let me go. I am sick and weary. Have some respect for an old woman.'

Kybele grasped the hands of the ancient goddess even more tightly. 'Please, Hekate, give me a salve, a temporary cure. Give something from the pouch of sweet and bitter herbs that you wear by your waist. I am only asking you this one thing. Did I ask you when Attis bled his lifeblood into the soil from the wound he himself had made? My grief was no less great, but this time it is different.'

'How so?' Hekate snapped. 'There is nothing different in this world. It is all the same, again and again and again.'

A certain coldness came over Kybele's face. She looked up at Hekate. 'It is different,' she said, 'because I wish to cheat Apollo of a prize taken by subterfuge.'

Kybele felt Hekate's hands soften. 'Why did you not tell me before?' the old crone asked. 'If your quarrel is with Apollo, then I will help you. Now, where is the thieving satyr?'

Kybele looked up at Hekate's lined face and smiled at her. 'Follow your nose,' she said.

Hekate sniffed the air like a hunting dog. Kybele took her by the arm, and led her to the scorched earth where Marsyas lay. The lions were sitting nearby, heads on their paws, watching the satyr for signs of life. They did not love Marsyas, but they sensed Kybele's love, and kept watch over him for her sake.

Hekate came to a stop near the place where Marsyas was lying and squatted down on her haunches. The old goddess examined him. She could sense the life in him struggling to free itself from the flesh.

'There is life in him,' Hekate said, 'but he wishes to die.'

'He must not.' Kybele's voice was calm and determined.

'He may curse you for saving his life,' Hekate said.

'I would rather live with his curse than suffer his death.'

Hekate rummaged in her pouch and pulled out a handful of herbs. She rubbed the herbs between her hands and spat on them for lubrication. The plants soon broke down into a dark, pulpy mash that she spread over her palms. Then she leaned down and put both palms on Marsyas's shoulders. The satyr's body flinched. His breathing became more audible. The toes of his left foot flexed.

Hekate closed her eyes and muttered to herself. She started to move her hands over the satyr's poor, raw body. As if scalded, Marsyas's flesh fluttered underneath her touch. She ran her hands over the chest, the belly, the groin with its raw and flaccid cock, the legs. Turning the little satyr over, she worked on his back. Marsyas, half conscious, dreamed he was burning in pitch. In his dreams he was screaming, but no sound came from his lips.

Hekate finished her work. She wiped her hands clean on her tunic. Marsyas was breathing more steadily now. His chest was visibly rising and falling.

As the satyr's strength and consciousness began to return, the pain—which had not been gone during his unconsciousness, but which was for a while running far underground, made subterranean—rose to the surface again, like a river breaking from the earth. A bleat of distress passed his lips. He rolled his head to one side. Kybele had to resist the impulse to reach out and comfort him. The longing to touch, and the knowledge that it would only cause Marsyas greater agonies, made her heart ache.

Hekate stood up. 'He will live,' she said, 'but he will not thank you for it. Take my advice. If you care for his sufferings, find him a skin.'

Then the old woman looked around through the gloom. 'Who has got my torch?' she snapped.

The little satyr who was holding her torch scampered over. Hekate took it without thanks. Then she turned and hobbled off across the hillside in the dark.

The light of her torch glimmered for a long time in the distance, then it dwindled to a pinprick of light and was gone.

27

Before the dawn broke, Kybele entrusted Marsyas to the care of several nymphs, and she departed for Olympos. The sky was filling with light as she climbed the broad highway of stars that led into the heavens. By the time the sun had come up over Phrygia, she had already passed through the Gate of Clouds and swept through the bronzed colonnade onto the sacred mountaintop. She paused to catch her breath in the sparse, scrubby courtyard. At the far end of the courtyard, towards the east, stood Zeus's throne room. She could hear the sound of metal being honed and shaped, coming from Hephaistos's forge.

Kybele had always hated Olympos. There was no surer sign of the idiocy of the Olympians than their prizing of elevation over expanse. The higher one climbs a mountain, the less room there is to move. Kybele loved the vast plains where grain turned golden in the summer sun. But she hated the cramped little hamlet that the Olympians called home. No amount of white marble and gleaming bronze could disguise the dismal narrowness of the place. It was stultifying. There were no seasons: no burning sun in summer, no cooling rain in autumn, no snows and chill winds in winter, no fresh, strong breezes in the spring. Nothing ever changed, other than the quarrels and the rivalries and the bickering. Whenever she visited, Kybele found herself gasping for breath. Whenever she departed the mountain, she felt as if she had been left somehow unclean.

Kybele hurried across the courtyard to the marble and bronze palace where she knew she would find Zeus upon his throne. The bronze doors were open. To either side of the doors were pillars on which were engraved images of the old man's conquests. Here he appeared as an eagle, lifting the pissing Ganymedes to the skies. Here he was a shower of gold, falling into the lap of Danae. Here he was a swan with broad, white wings, coupling with Leda.

Kybele stepped into the dark. The sickly sweetness of the air caught at the back of her throat. At the far end of the throne room she could see, half in shadow, the chief of the gods. He was sitting on his throne, dressed in a stained robe that covered only the lower part of his body. He was quite alone, plunging his sticky hands into a bronze pot full of pallid ambrosia, pulling out handfuls and cramming them into his mouth. Kybele could see the redness around his eyes, betraying the sleepless vigilance that comes with kingship. She had no love for him, but she pitied him.

'Kybele,' Zeus said when he saw her approach. He wiped his mouth clean with the back of his hand. 'It is early. What brings you to Olympos?'

'I have come to ask you for something,' Kybele said.

'A request? But first you must eat. Here . . .' Zeus reached into the pot and pulled out a quivering, whitish handful of ambrosia.

'No, thank you. My request is urgent. We cannot waste time. I have come about the satyr Marsyas.'

'Marsyas?' Zeus spluttered as he chewed on his ambrosia. 'The name is familiar, although I cannot say why.'

'The Phrygian satyr.'

'Ah, yes. The one with the pipe?'

'He has been punished by Apollo,' Kybele said. 'He lies stripped of his skin, like a sword drawn from its scabbard.'

Zeus waved a hand in the air in a gesture of vague irritation. 'Kybele, the world is full of men and satyroi. How can one keep track of them all?'

'Marsyas is dear to me.'

'A satyr? How can a piece of goat meat be dear to an immortal?'

'When men make sacrifice, you like the stench of goat meat well enough,' Kybele said.

Zeus smiled and put his ambrosia pot to one side. He wiped his hands on his tunic. His voice became conciliatory. 'But he has angered the gods,' he said. 'You cannot blame Apollo.'

'Has he committed any offence?'

'He has placed himself higher than the gods.'

Kybele sighed. It was always about height. 'Are gods higher than mortals in all things?' she asked.

Zeus gave a nervous laugh. 'Well, of course we are,' he said.

'Even death?'

'Ah, death,' said Zeus. Kybele was right. The mortals knew death the way that the immortals never could. And knowing death, they knew time. And knowing time, they had knowledge of life. And having knowledge of life, they had knowledge of all things.

'I have not come to quibble,' Kybele said. 'I ask only that the cruelty Marsyas has suffered be eased.'

'He lies without a skin, you say?'

'Yes, but he still lives. Hekate has seen to him with her herbs and ointments.'

'And this satyr's skin: where is it now?'

'It is in Apollo's hands. I have come to ask for it to be returned.'

Zeus raised his eyebrows. 'But Kybele, it was surrendered in a contest, and was rightfully taken from him.'

Kybele thought that there was a tremor of fear in Zeus's voice at the mention of Apollo's name. 'Zeus,' she said, 'you know the cruelty of Apollo as I do. I am merely asking that you keep this cruelty in check. He is testing it on satyroi and on men, as a swordsmith works a blade on a whetstone. It if continues unchecked, who is to say where it will end?'

'But Kybele,' Zeus said uneasily, 'let us not provoke Apollo's anger. You know the law: what one god has done no other may undo.'

'Who legislates this law, Zeus? I do not recognise it.'

'It is the way of things,' Zeus said. 'It has always been so.'

'Where I come from,' said Kybele, 'there is not this obsession with laws.'

'Where you come from there is much that is lacking,' Zeus said.

Kybele stared out of the window. She looked down the slopes of Olympos towards the sea, then to the east where Marsyas lay. 'My friend is in pain,' she said. 'I want you to end his pain. That is all I ask.'

'I cannot return his skin, but I can offer you a lesser recompense. It would not offend the heavens if you clothed that satyr of yours in another skin. If you do this, I will guarantee that Apollo does not interfere.'

'Thank you, Zeus.'

'And now, Kybele, I wish for something in return,' Zeus said.

Kybele could recognise a child-like hunger in Zeus's eyes.

'I am so tired of ambrosia,' the god said.

The goddess sighed. 'Then come,' she said.

The goddess unlaced her tunic and stepped towards the bearded god. Zeus leaned forward hungrily and put his red lips to Kybele's brown nipple. He clasped the breast with his rough hands, sticky with ambrosia, and he suckled hungrily. The goddess gazed out of the window and thought of Marsyas.

When Zeus had drunk his fill, he lifted his head. Kybele laced up her tunic, and he did not meet her eyes. Without saying another word, the goddess turned and left the palace. She headed back across the courtyard, through the Gate of Clouds and away from Olympos.

It was good to feel the breeze again, to smell the air heavy with the scents of late autumn, to be rid of the sticky sweetness of Olympos. Kybele hurried back to Phrygia where she stripped naked and bathed herself in the sparkling waters of the river Meander. Refreshed, she hurried back to Marsyas.

28

By the time Kybele returned, the valley was loud with morning birdsong. Marsyas lay, surrounded by nymphs and satyroi, like a goat carcass in a butcher's shop. Only from close-by was it possible to see his raw flesh shudder with rise and fall of his breath.

'I am here,' Kybele said. 'Do not worry. Your agony will not be long. We will find a new coat for you, Marsyas.'

'Let me die,' the satyr whispered.

'It will soon be over,' the goddess said.

Kybele turned away and gestured to one of the satyroi. 'Summon your tribe,' she said. 'As many as you can. We have work to do.' Then she said to one of the nymphs, 'Look after him. We will return.'

The little goatling scampered a little way up the slope of Tmolos and perched himself upon a jagged rock that overlooked the valley. There he let out a series of bleats: *meh-heee, meh-heee, meh-heee*. Hearing his call, from out of the nooks and crevices and gorges emerged clusters of satyroi. They came puffing and panting towards where Kybele stood. In a few moments, there had gathered a small crowd of around forty goatlings.

The goddess clicked her fingers. 'Come this way,' she said, and she led the satyr troop away across the fragrant meadows down to the lower slopes. They clustered behind her, whispering anxiously to each other. 'What's happening?' they asked. 'What does she want from us? Where are we going?'

They stopped in a meadow in the centre of which was a lovely little copse. Some way off, a single rabbit hunched, twitching its nose, watching them. Kybele gathered the satyroi around her. 'Friends,' she said, 'there are rabbits to hunt. Kill all you can, and we will make a new coat for your friend Marsyas. I will meet you here again at noon.'

The rabbit hopped away to its burrow. When the satyrs looked around the meadow, they saw that the ground was pockmarked with holes.

Kybele left them to their task. First the satyroi gathered rocks and stones. Then they pulled down branches and stripped them to use as clubs. And when they had everything they needed, they set to work. They spread out across the meadow. They squatted down by the rabbit burrows and farted into the warrens to drive the rabbits out. When the rabbits poked out their heads, the satyroi swung their clubs, and walloped and bashed with their rocks. And as they did so, they sang:

Club them, beat them, smash their brains,
till not a single one remains.
come decimate the rabbit tribe—
the weather's good for genocide.

May lagomorphic terror reign,
may bucks and kits and does be slain,

we'll bash and batter, bruise and beat,
until the massacre's complete.

May rabbit bodies stack and stack
we'll pile them high and haul them back,
and stitch a furry lapine coat,
to lay upon the new-peeled goat.

Come decimate the rabbit tribe—
the weather's good for genocide,
the weather's good for genocide.

The satyroi had not needed to kill quite so many rabbits; but once they started, the killing was so much fun that it was hard to stop. By the time Kybele returned at noon, a stinking pile of rabbit carcasses was heaped in the middle of the meadow. A stench of death and blood and flatulence hung on the air. Kybele sighed. She gathered the satyroi together, and gave them their orders.

After the fun of the killing, there was heavy work to do. The satyroi selected the least mangled carcasses—they had performed their task with more enthusiasm than skill—and carried them in armfuls to the clearing where Marsyas lay. The satyroi washed the dead rabbits in the river of tears, then they stripped off the skins and scraped them clean. The heap of pelts that they accumulated would have been enough to reskin half of the satyroi in Phrygia. Word soon spread, and nearby villagers soon appeared, coming over the hillside carrying baskets that they filled with rabbit flesh.

Kybele sorted through the skins, trying to select the best and most beautifully coloured. Many of the skins were so torn and hacked about that they were worthless. Kybele worked quickly. She selected sixty of the finest skins and bundled them into a sack. Then she set out across the hillside to a hut not far off where a shepherd lived with his wife. The woman, she knew, was skilled with the needle. Kybele gave her instructions and left the skins with her, saying she would return by sunset.

When she returned, she found that the old woman had done a good job. Kybele held up the rabbit-fur satyr suit and examined it closely. It was not perfect: the skins were patchy and mottled. But it was sturdy and well shaped, a row of rabbit-leather bows down the front to act as fastenings.

The old woman would not take payment. She had heard about what had happened to the satyr, and it pleased her that she could do something to help. As Kybele left, the old woman went to rummage in the corner, and brought out a flask of wine. 'Give this to the satyr,' she said. 'It might ease his pains a little.'

Kybele thanked the old woman and returned to where Marsyas lay. She put down the flask of wine, then she took some water from the stream and poured it over the satyr's trembling flesh. When he was clean, very carefully, she started to ease Marsyas into the suit.

The robing was no less painful than the disrobing, but the pain of each was different and distinct. Kybele pulled the suit onto Marsyas's legs. She tucked his raw cock into the little pouch at the groin. It looked strange, because the old woman had made the pouch bigger than it was needed when the cock was small, to give it room to expand. As a result, the pouch hung down between his legs like an empty purse. Next, Kybele forced the satyr to sit up and tugged the top half over his torso. Pulling the suit over his arms was agonising. Finally, Kybele pulled the suit together at the front by Marsyas's chest, and tied it closed with the bows, from top to bottom.

Marsyas was reclothed. He opened his eyes and saw Kybele's eyes looking back at him, blazing with kindness. He wriggled inside his new skin, moved his legs and his arms. And it was then that he realised, to his astonishment, that the pain was gone.

29

Kybele helped the satyr stand up. He got to his feet carefully, as if the pain might come flooding back at any time. But there was no pain. There was only a little stiffness and discomfort, as if he had suffered no more than a night sleeping badly on the valley floor.

Marsyas looked down at his new pelt. He frowned and ran his fingers through the fur as if to ask, 'Is this mine?'

Kybele reached out and touched him. He did not flinch. 'Marsyas,' she said. 'How is the pain?'

'Gone,' he said softly. He noticed an itch on his arm. He scratched at it. The itch moved further towards his shoulder. He scratched again.

'No pain,' he said. 'But I have an itch.'

'Marsyas,' said Kybele. 'Come here.' She put her arms round the satyr and hugged him close to her. Marsyas nuzzled into her breasts. The itch raced up his arm and down to his shoulder blade. And although the pain was gone, he couldn't get comfortable. Parts of his suit felt saggy, others were too tight. He wanted his skin back.

'Kybele,' he asked, 'where is my skin?'

'On Olympos,' the goddess told him. 'Apollo has it.'

At the mention of the god's name, Marsyas shuddered 'Then whose skin is this?'

'Rabbits,' Kybele said.

The satyr ran his fingers through his new fur. *Rabbits*? he thought.

'I want to look at myself,' Marsyas said.

'Follow the river downstream,' said Kybele. 'To the side of the river there is a pool where you can gaze at yourself.'

Marsyas could not remember there being a river. He wriggled free from Kybele's embrace, scratching at himself here and there, and looked at the tumbling watercourse that had sprung from the mourners' tears.

'Go on,' said Kybele. 'Do not be afraid. I will be waiting for you. You are safe, Marsyas.'

The satyr headed downstream until he came to the pool. He crouched down and gazed into the water. For a moment, he did not recognise the figure staring back, this forlorn clown in a loose-fitting skin, this sorrowful buffoon. *How can this be me?* he wondered. But the lips of the creature in the pool moved along with his own and the creature grimaced when Marsyas grimaced; it raised its eyebrows when Marsyas raised his eyebrows; it stuck out his tongue when the satyr stuck out his.

When Marsyas could bear to look no longer, he stood up and trailed back upstream to where Kybele was waiting.

The goddess picked Marsyas up and held him in her arms. 'I want my skin back,' the satyr moaned.

'I know, Marsyas. But this skin will have to do.'

'It itches,' he said. The itch had moved down towards his

lower back. Marsyas reached round to scratch it, but it scuttled away at the last moment, back up to his shoulder blade.

'You will get used to it. Here, have some wine.'

She took the flask of wine that the old woman had given her, tipped back the satyr's chin and poured some into his open mouth. It tasted strange on his tongue. Marsyas swallowed. The wine seemed to help. 'More,' Marsyas said. Kybele tipped the flask a second time.

Soon the flask was dry. Marsyas snuggled in the arms of the goddess. The itching was still there, but it didn't seem so bad when drunk. The worst thing was the memory of the pain, looming over him the way a great cliff or a mountain blots out the sun. He tried to turn his mind away from it. 'Kybele,' he said, 'tell me a story.'

To distract him from his sufferings, Kybele told Marsyas a tale from the time of the Titans, and Marsyas nestled against her and closed his eyes. Soon he was asleep.

Kybele put the sleeping satyr down on the ground. As she gazed down at him, she was struck by the terrible realisation that the Marsyas she had loved was gone. She had loved the Marsyas who dreamed of music, the Marsyas who had the audacity to challenge Apollo, the Marsyas who trembled when her lions stirred, who frolicked and played. This creature was something different, and she didn't love it in the same way. There was a lingering affection for the thing. Her heart suffered to see its sufferings. But she did not love it.

The goddess tiptoed away.

When he woke the following dawn, Kybele was no longer there. Marsyas rubbed his eyes and squinted into the daylight. He had been dreaming peaceful dreams, but the moment he awoke the memories returned. The first nick of Hermes's knife. The music of Apollo's lyre. The way the skin had been peeled away from his flesh. Marsyas shuddered.

The itching was there again. When he scratched, it made it worse. It was as if scratching made his skin slide just a little over the flesh beneath. The sensation was horrible.

I need a nymph, he told himself. A nymph will help me forget. A nymph will take my mind off things. He padded across the hillside and, when he found a place where the trees grew more thickly, he plunged into the undergrowth.

He had not gone far when he heard the sound of laughter. The little satyr scampered over to take a look, and there he saw them: a small group of nymphs bathing in a pool in a woodland clearing. They were perfectly naked, their robes heaped in a bundle on the bank, and they were splashing water over each other. Marsyas smiled to himself and felt his cock rise in its pouch. There was something disagreeable in the sensation but, trying to make the best of things, he satyr scampered out of the bushes and let out a bleat of with desire.

The nymphs looked up. They started to giggle. Marsyas's rabbitskin cock—furry to the very end—looked like a leaping weasel. The tallest of the nymphs pointed and laughed. She climbed out of the water, her long legs bronze in the sunlight. Then, quite naked, she held her sides and she shook with mocking laughter.

Marsyas looked down at the skin that was not his own, shabby and badly fitting. And it was then that he realised that he was no longer beautiful. His cock shrank back, the half empty pouch dangling between his thighs. Marsyas turned and ran back into the bushes. The itching seemed to be everywhere now—on his belly, his neck, his back, his legs, his balls.

The little satyr started to run, heading through the woods blindly, as if he could outstrip the appalling itching. But the itching followed him. He gasped and flailed as he ran, scratching at himself until he stumbled over a tree root and tumbled down a slope into a ditch.

Marsyas curled himself into a ball, and he cried.

What is the best thing?
To never have been born.
What is the second best?
To die soon.

30

The winter that year was colder than anybody could remember. Marsyas spent his days in the hut of an old shepherd. For most of the dark winter months, he simply stared into the fire and scratched at himself. He had no appetite for anything. Sometimes his satyr brethren came calling and tried to rekindle in him an enthusiasm for life. 'Cheer up,' they said. 'It's not as bad as all that! Don't mope! Have some cheese!' But when Marsyas did not respond, they left him to his brooding.

In the spring, Marsyas moved back out into the hills. He kept his own company, brooding and scratching in the solitude of shady ravines and mountain caves. It sometimes seemed to him as if he was waiting for something, but he was not sure what.

As the spring turned to summer, and the weather became hotter, the itching got worse. Marsyas found that it helped a little to plunge himself into the mountain streams and let the chill waters soothe him. Sometimes he could be seen—a goatish head with closed eyes in the middle of the stream, his entire body immersed. Wagtails and dippers, imagining he was a rock, perched on his head to rest.

*

Towards the next autumn, strange rumours from the east started to reach Phrygia, tales of a vast army making its way westwards. People whispered of terror and upheaval; of sheep, horses, men and goats torn apart by half naked women; of strange couplings on the hillsides; of wine and song and joy and despair. The Phrygian satyroi, excited by these rumours, climbed to the peaks and looked towards the horizon, trying to spot the oncoming army. But Marsyas kept his own company. He felt a stirring of unease in the base of his belly.

Then, one overcast morning, a terrible buzzing could be heard over the mountainside, the sound of ten thousand bull-roarers. The ground started to shake. A little later, the hills turned black with swarming figures. And at the head of this great army was a figure brandishing a staff fashioned of a fennel stalk and topped by a pinecone.

It was Dionysos, burned by the sun, returning in triumph from India. If he had left Phrygia as a lunatic child, his mind like a cracked pot, now he was returning as a creature fully god. And behind him was a retinue, a rabble of satyroi and seilenoi, gymnosophists and soma-eaters, shramanas and vratyas, merry pranksters and musicians, ascetics, korybantes, hangers-on and sundry pilgrims.

Kybele heard the sound of their approach. She stood on the mountainside and watched them swarm into the valley, where they started to set up camp.

So, Dionysos has returned, she thought.

31

As darkness fell, the fires of Dionysos's followers lit the skies with red for miles around. There was drinking and celebration. And on that night, ten thousand human children were conceived, and five thousand creatures of mixed origin—animal, godling or human, depending upon the proportions of blood and ichor that flowed in their veins.

Seeing that his followers were well settled and had no need of him, Dionysos crept away to find the goddess Kybele. He found her in the quiet grove where they had first met. Her lions were asleep in the moonlight. The surge of voices in the valley, muffled by the trees, sounded like the swell of the sea. And although he came to Phrygia in triumph, like a great general, when he stood before the goddess, Dionysos seemed small and timid. He kept his head lowered, and waited for the goddess to speak first.

'Dionysos,' she said, 'Welcome.' She reached out and lifted his chin. She looked into his eyes, and knew that he was no longer the youth he once had been. He had the scent of wine on his breath.

'Thank you,' said Dionysos.

The two of them embraced.

'Dionysos,' Kybele said, 'There is much I have to tell you.' She gestured to a nearby rock and Dionysos sat down. It was soft with moss and served as a comfortable enough couch. Kybele smiled. 'But first, tell me of India,' she said.

Dionysos sighed in the way that youths returning from the East have always sighed. 'There is too much to tell, Kybele,' he said. 'In India, the name of Zeus is unknown and Apollo is nothing. I have never seen such luxury or such poverty, such joy or such suffering.'

Kybele nodded. 'And on your return you bring an army, I see?' she smiled.

Dionysos gave a broad, easy smile. 'I bring no army,' he said. 'I issue no commands. These people follow me after their own volition. I do not ask for followers, yet I find myself followed. But soon I will leave them, because I have business on Olympos.'

Kybele was surprised. 'Olympos? What business do you have on Olympos? You are not born for such a place, Dionysos.'

'I wish to claim my place as a god. It is my birthright. I am born of the seed of Zeus.'

'And your followers?'

'They will disperse after I have gone. If you fear having so many mouths to feed here in Phrygia . . .'

'I fear nothing, Dionysos. There is grain enough in Phrygia. They may stay or leave, according to their wishes.'

'Thank you, Kybele.'

Kybele smiled. 'How long will you be staying?'

Dionysos looked down at the ground. 'Before Olympos, I must pay a visit to the underworld. My mother, Semele, is down in Hades. I will fetch her from the darkness, and take her with me to Olympos.'

Kybele looked astonished. 'How do you propose to get to Hades?'

'That I do not know,' the god said. 'What can an immortal know of the world of the dead?'

'Here I cannot help you,' said Kybele. 'But I know who can.'

'Who?' asked the god.

'Marsyas,' Kybele said. 'The satyr who saved you from your madness.'

Dionysos frowned. 'That little satyr? What does he know?'

'He has spoken with Orpheus.'

'Orpheus?' Dionysos looked a little ashamed.

'Is it true what they say: that he was torn apart by the women of your retinue?'

Dionysos opened his palms wide. 'As I have told you, Kybele, I issue no commands. What others do is their concern.'

Kybele inclined her head. 'Well, then. Orpheus is one of the few amongst men who have been to the underworld and returned,' she said. 'The satyr met with him whilst at sea. He was in poor shape—just his head, nothing else, but still capable of song and speech. They talked of the underworld. Go and speak with Marsyas. He will know more.'

'I will do so,' said the god.

PART V
UNDERWORLD

32

Marsyas was alone by the riverbank. Kingfishers and shimmering dragonflies darted around him, but he did not pay them any attention. He was lying on his belly and staring at the ground, watching a column of marching ants go about some obscure insect mission or other.

Dionysos came quietly towards the river, so as not to startle the satyr. The shabby figure was unrecognisable to him. The dazzling god sat down beside Marsyas and reached out a hand to touch his arm. 'Marsyas,' he said.

The satyr did not reply, nor did he look round. Instead he reached a hand down to his side and scratched at himself.

'Marsyas,' the god said again. 'It is your friend, Dionysos.'

Marsyas recognised the voice, but he could not bring himself to reply.

'How have you been? I can see you have suffered. I have heard about what Apollo did.'

Marsyas leaned forward, fixing his attention on the marching line of ants.

'I have not forgotten what you did for me in my madness,

Marsyas,' the god said. 'I have not forgotten, and I would like to reward you.'

For the first time Marsyas looked up. The god had always been beautiful, but now that he had returned from India, he was more beautiful still. The god's beauty made Marsyas feel drab and gloomy. 'What reward?' the satyr asked, his voice a monotone.

'Your skin, Marsyas,' said Dionysos. 'I can help you get back your skin.'

Marsyas scratched himself again on the back, feeling the discomfort of his new skin slipping against his flesh. 'It itches, Dionysos,' he said.

The god looked at him. 'I can help you,' he repeated.

'But how, Dionysos? What one god has done . . .' The itch scuttled up his spine like the column of ants.

'Marsyas, your suffering is not inevitable,' the god said. 'It is true that I cannot give you back your skin, for I too am a god. But there is no law against a *mortal* undoing that which a god has done.'

Marsyas's eyes open wide. 'Dionysos, don't torment me,' he said. 'My skin is up on Olympos. How can I, a mortal, ascend to those heights?'

Dionysos smiled. 'That's easy,' he said. 'You can accompany me.'

A flock of small finches settled in a bush not far away, and started to strip it bare of seeds. They finished their task and flew away. 'No,' the satyr said, shaking his head.

'They say,' Dionysos said, 'that whenever Apollo plays his lyre, your skin quivers.'

'I cannot go,' Marsyas whispered. 'Apollo will recognise me. He will destroy me.'

'Apollo does not even know that you are alive,' Dionysos

said. 'And who would recognise you in that coat you are wearing? What is it made of, by the way?'

'Rabbits,' Marsyas mumbled.

Dionysos laughed. 'Marsyas, do not overestimate the gods. Even if you stood on Olympos before Apollo and cried out "I'm Marsyas!", looking like that, he would not believe you.'

Marsyas tugged at the loose folds of his skin. 'If I get my skin back,' he said, 'what then? Where do I go? What do I do? Wait for another flaying?'

'There will be no more flayings. I will take you to India. There, beyond the Tigris and the Euphrates and the Indus, you will be safe.'

'Surely Apollo will find me.'

'India is beyond his jurisdiction. They have other gods in India. I have friends there. I can guarantee your safety.'

'Apollo will seek me out. He will destroy me.'

Dionysos laughed. 'Do not believe all you are told, Marsyas. The gods of Olympos are not rulers of the world. There is only one creature that rules the world.'

'Man?' the satyr asked.

Dionysos laughed again. 'Man does not even rule himself,' he said. 'How can he be said to rule the world?'

Then he reached down and picked up a single ant. It ran over the back of his brown hand and sniffed the air with its antennae. Dionysos put it back on the ground, and it scurried back into formation. 'The ant, Marsyas, is the true ruler of the world. When compared with the vast empires and cities of the ants, men and gods are nothing.'

Marsyas looked down at the marching column of ants. He imagined that this must be how the Olympians gazed down upon the lives of men. He leaned over and squashed a single ant with his thumb. He felt neither compassion nor remorse nor joy. He wondered if this, too, must be what it is like to be a god. The satyr scraped the crushed body of the ant from his thumb on the grass. 'Tell me about India,' he said.

So Dionysos told him about the great river Ganga. He told him about the mountains that towered higher even than Olympos. He told him about the strange and powerful gods who knew nothing of Zeus, Apollo and Aphrodite. And he told him about the women and boys skilled in the arts of desire.

'But Dionysos,' Marsyas said, looking down at his shabby coat. 'Who would desire me now?'

'You forget, Marsyas. You will be returned to your own skin. It is there on Olympos, on a peg in Apollo's chambers. So let us not waste any time. We go to Olympos, you reclaim your skin, and I take you to India before Apollo even knows you have gone.'

The satyr sat up and propped his chin on his knees. The itch was now crawling across his chest. 'And the itch?' he asked.

'When you are returned to your skin, you will itch no more.'

Marsyas thought for a while. He could sit out his days and months and years itching and scratching at his ill-fitting skin. Or he could journey with Dionysos to Olympos. And after that, India.

'I'll come,' he said.

The god patted Marsyas on the thigh. 'Good,' he said. 'We leave tomorrow.'

Marsyas felt a peculiar stirring inside him. Sometimes this is how hope arrives, like a god winched down from above the stage on some rickety crane. And if this is how it chooses to arrive, why should it be refused?

'There is only one thing,' said Dionysos. 'We will need to make a diversion on the way, and for this I need your assistance.'

Marsyas hesitated. 'A diversion?' he asked. 'Where?'

'Hades, Marsyas.'

Marsyas leaned forward, eyes wide. 'Hades?' he whispered.

'Hades,' Dionysos said. 'My mother is down there. I want to fetch her and take her back to Olympos. And I will need you as a guide.'

'But what do I know of Hades?'

'First, you are a satyr, and so you are skilled in finding paths and tracks. Secondly, you spoke with Orpheus about the journey to Hades, and he told you many things that may be of use to us. Take me to the places that Orpheus told you about. Let us go together.' He patted Marsyas on the arm.

When Marsyas looked at Dionysos more closely, he noticed something strange. The god had paled just a little. His lips were trembling, his eyes wavering. It was then that Marsyas realised that Dionysos was *afraid*.

'My poor mother,' the god sighed. 'She has been in that terrible place for years.'

Marsyas gave the god a sly look. 'The ghosts must be sending her out of her mind,' he said.

Dionysos blanched a little more. 'Ghosts?' he asked. 'I had not thought about ghosts. Will there be ghosts?'

Seeing the god's fear, Marsyas himself felt a surge of bravery. There is nothing like the terror of another for stirring up courage. 'Yes,' he said. 'And demons, as well, I'd imagine.'

'Demons?' Dionysos seemed to be breaking out in a kind of godly sweat.

'And lost souls. The terrible things I've heard, Dionysos, they would make your hair stand on end . . .'

Dionysos stood up. 'Enough, Marsyas!' he said, his voice curiously strained. 'We leave tomorrow. I am counting on you.'

The god scuttled away into the trees.

Marsyas sat watching the march of the ants. He could feel his courage mounting. Yes, he thought, reclaiming his skin would be a small matter. He would lead Dionysos through the underworld. From Hades they would travel up to Olympos. And there he would reclaim what was rightfully his. Then, reclothed in his skin, he would flee to the East, far from Apollo's reach.

For the first time since his flaying, Marsyas smiled.

33

The following morning Dionysos was waiting at the appointed place, pacing back and forth. Marsyas appeared out of the forest and scampered to the god's side. 'I am ready,' he said. He was almost cheerful, even though the itching still troubled him.

'Come, then,' said Dionysos. 'It is a long journey ahead of us.'

They set off in the direction of the northwest, heading first for Thrace. Dionysos went ahead and Marsyas tagged along behind. On the way, they took advantage of the hospitality of goatherds and villagers. They drank wine, and ate peasant bread and cheese. Were it not for the itching of his flesh, Marsyas might have found the journey a pleasure. But the irritation kept him awake at night, and when he woke in the mornings, his legs felt heavy.

They crossed the water into Thrace and made their way into the mountains. After struggling over rocky outcrops and wandering through beautiful upland meadows carpeted with flowers, they came to a place where the pine trees grew as thickly as a man's beard. 'This is it,' Marsyas said. 'I recognise it from Orpheus's description. It must be around here somewhere.'

Now Marsyas went ahead. He followed the line of a stream down hill towards a deep ravine. Dionysos lagged behind. As they plunged into the ravine, the sun slipped out of sight behind the mountains. It was suddenly cold. 'Are you sure this is the way?' Dionysos called, a tremor in his voice.

'This is it,' Marsyas said. 'Have you lost your nerve?'

Marsyas liked being on the trail of something. It helped him forget the raw tickling of his flesh. It made him believe that maybe things were going to be all right. But the god's face was pallid. 'Dionysos,' the satyr said, 'you look pale. You're not scared, are you?'

'No,' said Dionysos quietly. But when the god reached out a hand to steady himself on the path, Marsyas saw that he was shaking.

'Dionysos,' Marsyas said, 'when Orpheus was telling me about underworld, he mentioned something about snakes . . .'

Dionysos stopped. 'Snakes? There are *snakes* in Hades? You're not just trying to scare me?'

Marsyas looked innocent. 'I'm just passing on what Orpheus told me, so that we might be better prepared.'

Dionysos's lower lip started to quiver a bit. 'What else did Orpheus say?'

'There was the something about slime marshes—they didn't sound very nice. And he said that the underworld is filled with the *worst* sort of people. Monsters, too. I can't remember what kind, but they were terrifying, all teeth and fangs. In fact, the things that Orpheus told me—they'd make you shit yourself.' Marsyas grinned at the trembling god. 'Anyway,' he said, 'we can't waste time chatting. Are you coming?'

The satyr continued down the ravine. The god followed behind. The stream fell steeply until they came to a crevice, slippery with moss, where the water entered the earth. Marsyas crouched down before the opening and stuck his head inside the hole. 'Yoohoo!' he called.

The cavern boomed back at him. The satyr popped his head out. 'It's dark in there,' he said.

'Are there bats?' Dionysos asked.

'Hundreds,' said Marsyas. 'Thousands, probably. Come on. Let's go!'

Then he clambered down into the darkness, and Dionysos had no choice other than to follow.

Inside the cave was a stone path, no more than a foot wide, curving out of sight into the darkness. To one side of the path a cliff plunged down into the ravine where the waters raged. To the other side was a cold, sheer wall, oozing dampness. Marsyas went ahead, moving along the path with the confidence of a goat. Dionysos watched as Marsyas's back disappeared into the darkness. 'Hurry up!' Marsyas called. His voice was drowned out by the sound of the waterfall.

Dionysos followed behind on shaking legs. Every few steps he had to pause and catch his breath. Soon they had gone from the light, and were surrounded by darkness. The god could hear the twittering of bats. He pressed himself against the cliff and tried not to think of the drop behind him. 'Marsyas!' he shouted. 'Slow down!' But the words did not come out right, because his teeth were chattering. He clamped his jaws shut and kept moving, pace by pace.

But Marsyas was quickening his pace, following the path down into the depths of the earth. The further he went, the more he noticed that the itching of his flesh was subsiding, the edges taken off. There was something soothing about the darkness, something almost delicious. But it wasn't just the itching—it was *everything*. With every step it seemed that the whole of existence, with its mountains and valleys, was being flattened out. A strange indifference started to envelop the satyr.

'Keep going, Dionysos!' he called over his shoulder, and he plunged even further down the path.

Then he noticed something else. The memory of his former sufferings no longer pricked him as it had, nor did the memory of his former pleasures stir him. Everything had the same taste as everything else: stale, bland, but neither pleasant nor unpleasant. Marsyas put out his tongue and licked the wall of the cave. It, too, tasted of staleness, a subtle, lingering sadness.

A while later, Marsyas realised that the path had diverged from the subterranean river. He was moving on the same ledge through a soundless, muffled darkness. He could not hear Dionysos behind him, but he was sure that the god would catch up eventually. Occasionally a twittering shadow brushed past him. He shooed the shadows—whatever they were—away with his hand.

Later still, the blackness that surrounded him gave way to a grey pallor, the colour of smoke. The air was neither hot nor cold, but it had a kind of thickness, almost a stickiness. The path levelled out, opening onto a vast, grey plain. Through the gloom, Marsyas made out a glinting ribbon in the distance. It looked like a great body of water, overhung with a thick, greyish-brown mist. The hither bank was crowded with travellers, milling around with a distracted air, as if they had lost something but could not quite remember what. Marsyas scrabbled down the end of the path and then he stopped. He thought he should let Dionysos catch up, so he sat down on a boulder to wait.

In due course—it was impossible to say how long it took; it might have been an hour, or a month, or a year—he heard the god puffing and whimpering his way towards him down the path. Dionysos appeared from the darkness, white with fear. He sat down next to Marsyas and immediately started to sob. 'This is such a terrible place,' he said. 'We should not have come!'

Marsyas looked at the god with indifference. Things seemed empty, hollow, peaceful. Then the satyr pointed to the water. 'I think we need to go that way,' he said.

'The Styx,' Dionysos whispered. 'The river of hate.'

Just then they heard voices behind them. A procession of shadowy figures emerged out of the dark and hurried past in the direction of the water. There were ten or twelve of them in all. Six of them were bearing a corpse on their shoulders, wrapped in the cloths of mourning. It occurred to Marsyas that it was ostentatious to put on the airs and graces of a corpse in the underworld. After all, wasn't *everybody* dead?

'I wonder what they are up to,' said Marsyas. 'Let's follow them.'

The satyr took the god by the hand. It was cold and clammy. He led the god through the thick, stale air towards the water where the travellers and pilgrims were gathered. Some were alone, some huddled in small groups. They jostled and pressed up against each other, but pulled back from the dark, brackish waters. The mist was so thick and low that it was impossible to tell whether this was the bank of a river or the shore of a great sea. If there was a far bank, it was lost in the gloom. The satyr pulled Dionysos through the crowd until they reached the water's edge. He bent down and dipped a finger in the water to taste it. Had this been a river on earth, it would have been foul and acrid to the taste, but here it left him indifferent. He stood up again and looked into the mist.

'What do we do now?' Dionysos asked.

Marsyas pointed into the dark. 'That's what,' he said.

Dionysos looked out over the water. He saw the silhouette of a figure, standing in a boat. The figure was heading through the thick fog towards them.

34

The boat drifted towards the shore. It looked rickety—a few old planks roped together and sealed with black tar. Standing at the stern, punting with a long pole, was an old man in a grey cape. As the boat approached, a low moan went up from the cluster of souls on the bank. They jostled together on the shoreline, muttering and whispering.

Dionysos was almost overwhelmed with terror. 'It is Kharon,' he said. 'I have heard tell of Kharon.'

'Who?'

'The ferryman of the underworld. He is so terrifying that few even dare to speak his name.'

'He doesn't look terrifying to me,' Marsyas said. 'He's just some old timer trying to make a living. Or a dying. One or the other.' Then the satyr started to wave. 'Oi! Kharon! Over here!'

The ferryman, who was not used to being called by name, lifted his punting pole and let the boat drift towards the shore. The bow of the boat nudged at the muddy bank. Kharon sighed and stepped towards the bows. Marsyas was close enough to smell his breath. It smelled of despair. 'I'm Marsyas,' the satyr said. 'And this is Dionysos. Take us across.'

The boatman regarded them steadily. Then, with measured courtesy, he replied. 'You must wait your turn, Sirs. There's eternity ahead, so there's no need to hurry. And to tell the truth, I don't much like satyroi in the boat. Nothing but trouble. Only recently I was taking a Phoenician merchant across. He told me a terrible story about a satyr. Granted, the man was an idiot. He'd been stupid enough to fall in love with the beast, he said. And the satyr—well, to tell the truth, I'm not sure what happened, because I wasn't really listening. That's the trouble with this job. They all want to tell their stories . . .'

'Are you going to let us into your boat or not?' Marsyas asked.

'At least I only get stories half of the time,' the ferryman went on. 'The ferry is strictly one-way. I have my orders. The advantage is that I have the way back to myself. Keeps me sane, it does. I can have a bite to eat, watch the smoke over the river. I'd go mad without a bit of time to myself.' The boatman paused, his pole half out of the river of slime, as if he had lost his thread. 'But the point is this,' he said, 'I'm not taking the satyr. I'll take you, Sir, but the satyr will have to swim.'

Dionysos's lip trembled. The thought of going any further without Marsyas terrified him. 'Please, Kharon, the satyr is my guide. Let him come with me.'

'Guide? Oh, you are important, are you? Perhaps a ruler of some small country I haven't heard of? Or some kind of politician?'

'I am a god.' Dionysos said.

'I am sure you are, Sir.' The boatman gave a wan smile.

'I am the great Dionysos.'

'You are?' the old man said, as if he had heard it all before. 'Well, good for you.'

The corpses shuffling around on the riverbank looked at the god with a fleeting interest, then they looked away again. They had been shuffling and milling about for so long that nothing was particularly interesting to them. Kharon, leaned forward and studied Dionysos closely. 'Let me tell you, you're a pretty scrawny specimen for a god,' he said. 'Anyway, I don't care who you are. I suppose I can take you across, but you'll have to give me something nice to nibble on.'

Dionysos held up his open palms. 'I have nothing,' he said.

'No barley cakes placed in the grave? Most people bring those.'

'No,' Dionysos said. 'I am not dead.'

'Ah, well,' said Kharon. 'That's pretty bad luck.'

The ferryman ambled back to the stern and then he punted a little way further along the shore where an orderly group of souls had decided to form themselves into a queue of sorts. Kharon smiled at them. 'Hades, is it? All aboard for eternity. Barley cakes, arrowheads, jewellery, anything you have, just pop it in the bag here.'

The passengers embarked, handing over their grave goods. The queue shuffled forwards. Kharon and his passengers slipped away over the surface of the waters into the dark.

Not far from where Dionysos and Marsyas stood, there was a corpse. Perhaps it was the corpse that they had seen carried past them earlier. Or perhaps it was another corpse. Corpses look pretty much the same as each other. It was the corpse of a bearded man, wrapped up in his grave clothes, and it lay quietly on its back, looking up at the grey mist. 'Let us see if this fellow can help us out,' said Dionysos. He leaned over and tapped the body. 'You there,' he said, giving the body another prod, 'I want a word with you.'

With a rustling of grave clothes, the corpse sat up. 'What?' it asked.

'Have you any grave goods?'

'What kind of goods?'

'Barley cakes. Jewellery. Anything will do.'

The corpse looked at the god and shrugged. 'Why would I give them to you?' it asked.

The corpse was about to lie down again when Marsyas intervened. He grabbed the body by the winding cloths. 'Oi, stiff!' he said. 'Hold on a bit. We could do a trade.'

'What do you have?' asked the corpse.

'Marsyas!' Dionysos whispered. 'I do not like this.'

The satyr ignored him. 'The two of us are alive,' he said, pointing to himself and to Dionysos. 'Not dead. Alive. Do you understand what that means?'

'Nice for you,' said the corpse.

'What I'm saying,' the satyr whispered, 'is this: have you got any *messages*?'

'Messages? What for?'

'You know, for the living. You got a wife, for example?'

The corpse winced at the memory. 'I had one once. She was beautiful . . .' it said. Then it seemed to become a little vague and befuddled.

'Good,' said Marsyas. 'We'll take a message to her in exchange for a couple of barley cakes. What do you say?'

The corpse frowned with the effort of remembering. 'Her name is Eumelia,' the stiff said. 'She lives in Didyma. She is known for her singing voice. If you ask there, they will know her.'

'And the message?' asked Marsyas.

The corpse thought for a moment. 'Tell her that I always preferred my fish cooked more lightly.'

Marsyas hesitated. 'Are you *sure* that's the message?'

The corpse shrugged. 'She always cooked fish until they were dry. It's no way to cook a fish.'

'I'll tell her,' Marsyas said. 'Now, give me two barley cakes and we're quits.'

The corpse reached into its grave cloths and pulled out two barley cakes. 'Don't forget,' it whispered, before lying down and becoming corpse-like again.

From the river came the *splosh! splosh!* of Kharon's boat. Dionysos glanced at Marsyas, then looked at the corpse. The corpse was playing dead.

The boat emerged from the mist. Kharon's old, wavering voice called, 'Come along, all aboard. No slackers! Eternity can't wait. Ha! Ha! Come on you two! Don't dally! What have you got for me?'

Marsyas held up the barley cakes and dropped them into the boatman's bag. 'After you,' he said to the god.

The goatling and the trembling god climbed into the boat. Kharon pushed off from the bank and started to pole his ferry across the dark, still waters.

Dionysos felt ill at ease in the boat. The rickety craft and fetid river made him distinctly uncomfortable. He shifted his weight. As he shifted, the boat rocked dangerously. The more he shifted, the more the boat rocked; and the more the boat rocked, the more ill at ease he became, and the more he shifted.

Kharon soon lost his patience. 'You there!' he snapped.

'Who do you think you are? Sit on the cross-bench and don't move, or I'll toss you overboard.'

Meekly, Dionysos did as he was told.

Marsyas gazed out into the dark. Everything was hazy. Everything was unclear. The past and the future—Hermes's knife, the *aulos*, Kybele, Olympos, India—there in the underworld's eternal present, all these things seemed no more than vague dreams.

35

Kharon raised and lowered his pole, punting the boat through the mist. He was in no hurry. He had plenty of time. Dionysos and Marsyas listened to the splosh of the pole as Kharon dipped it in and out of the river. Strange phosphorescence glimmered in the water. Dionysos hugged his knees, teeth chattering. He tried not to shift around and unsettle the boat. He gazed across the misty darkness of the river, and as he did so, he heard voices in the distance. He held his breath. The voices were getting louder.

βρεκε-κεξ, κο-αξ, κο-αξ	*breke-kex, ko-ax, ko-ax*
κο-αξ, κο-αξ, κο-αξ!	*ko-ax, ko-ax, ko-ax*

Panicked, the god peered into the dark. 'What is *that*?' he asked, his eyes wide.

The sound came a second time.

βρεκε-κεξ, κο-αξ, κο-αξ	*breke-kex, ko-ax, ko-ax*
κο-αξ, κο-αξ, κο-αξ!	*ko-ax, ko-ax, ko-ax*

'Frogs,' Kharon said. 'Over there, in the reeds.'

Not far off, a small island of mud rose out of the river, and on the island was a cluster of reeds through which there whispered a slight breeze.

'Frogs?' Dionysos asked. 'You have frogs in the underworld?'

Kharon lifted his punting pole and let the boat drift. He pointed into the darkness. The god's eyes followed Kharon's long, bony finger. Just visible in the gloom was cluster of frogs, nestling in the dark beneath the reeds.

'What are they . . .' Dionysos started to ask. But he didn't finish the sentence, because at that moment the frogs erupted into song.

βρεκε-κεξ! Play the game!
κο-αξ, κο-αξ! Sink or swim!
Standing together or not.
It's all just the same,
when you're laid in your grave,
and your friends leave your body to rot.

All day in the bog,
what most pleases a frog
is to sit on his fat arse and croak;
but when he is dead,
then poor froggy is led,
down into the darkness and smoke.

So we croak till we croak,
but our croaking's not done,
for there's plenty more croaking to do!

We'll eternally croak,
for the recently croaked,
and sing Stygian frogsongs for you.

'Do you put up with this every day?' Dionysos asked.

'The frogs? Oh, they're not so bad,' Kharon said. 'Nice voices some of them.'

βρεκεκε-κεξ, don't complain,
κο-αξ, κο-αξ, don't be glum,
our frogsongs are fine and they're free . . .

But Dionysos, his nerves already strained, could not bear the singing any longer. He leaned over and called back over the dark, misty water—

Oh, desist and be still,
you amphibian bores.
Can't you let us all just R.I.P.?

Kharon pulled up his punting pole, and swung it at the god. It struck him across the back. It was not a mortal blow. It was more the kind of blow that a strict parent might use to reprimand a child. Dionysos let out a small cry and lurched to the side. The boat rocked. Marsyas grabbed hold of the god and the boat steadied again.

'Let that be a lesson,' said Kharon. Then he started to punt again.

These passengers, he thought, were discourteous, and he was not pleased. One of the pleasures of working with the dead was that they were usually unfailingly polite. The grave is a great education in good manners. But these two—they were unbearable.

The frogs resumed their song, but in the language of frogs.

βρεκε-κεξ, βρεκε-κεξ,
βρεκε-κεξ, βρεκε-κεξ,
βρεκε-κεξ, βρεκε-κεξ,
κο-αξ, κο-αξ!

When the boat reached the other side of the river, Kharon pulled in his punting pole and nodded to Dionysos and Marsyas.

'This is it?' Marsyas asked.

'This is it.'

The satyr got to his feet. 'Come on, Dionysos,' he said. 'We're here.'

But Kharon held up a hand. 'Two more barley cakes,' he said.

'Two more?' asked Marsyas.

'One for disembarkation tax, and one as a fine for insulting the frogs.'

Dionysos glanced at Marsyas. '*Quick*,' he hissed. '*Run!*'

The god and the satyr leapt from the boat onto the muddy bank, tumbling into the shallows with a splash. They struggled to the shore. Kharon raised his pole to give them another good whack, but they were already out of reach, struggling through the mud, up the slope and into the mist beyond.

The ferryman sighed. He turned his boat around and began to punt back across the Styx. Before long, he could hear the singing of the frogs again. Their batrachian warblings made his heart glad. He pulled in his pole, stowed it in the boat, and sat down to listen to their recital and munch on barley cakes.

When the frogs at last fell silent and the barley cakes were finished, Kharon brushed the last crumbs away. 'Thank you,' he called to the frogs, because it was always polite to thank them for a good recital. Then he stood and started to punt the boat back to the other shore.

36

Muddied and out of breath, Dionysos and Marsyas struggled up the slope to the ridge. They climbed all the way to the top and sat down. Side by side they looked out over the dark waters of the Styx. This bank was quieter than on the other side. Occasionally a group of shades drifted past, not stopping to chat, not causing anybody any trouble, not going anywhere in particular. Dionysos and Marsyas ignored them.

'Fucking frogs,' the god said.

Marsyas didn't reply. He plucked at the loose folds in his rabbit-skin coat. The itching had entirely gone now. He looked down at the pouch between his legs. It didn't seem to mean anything to him.

The mist started to come in from the river. Dionysos shivered and got to his feet. 'Come on, Marsyas,' he said. 'My mother is waiting.'

They made their way over the ridge of the hill. Soon after clearing the ridge, the ground became hard beneath their feet. The air became hotter, the mist more like steam. They walked until they came to a place where the rocks were riven with fissures. From out of the fissures jets of steam burst upwards into the thick hot air. There was a sulphurous smell. Marsyas went ahead, following the line of what looked like an ancient path. Dionysos hurried behind him.

A faint gleam of light appeared on the distant horizon. Marsyas headed in that direction. They walked for a long time until the darkness started to lift. Then Marsyas heard something, a snippet of a tune, the sound of a single-stemmed flute. He turned in the direction of the music. The ground started to slope downwards again. They followed the path down onto a broad, open plain where a meadow stretched into the distance, covered with flowers. The flowers were blue, yellow, red and purple, although they looked like they were covered by a fine layer of dust. Marsyas sniffed the air. It had the same stale, lifeless taste as before. He could not catch the scent of pollen.

'Where is the music coming from?' Dionysos had heard the flute too, and something about it set him on edge.

Marsyas narrowed his eyes. 'Look! There in the meadow.'

In the far distance was a column of people. At first they were no larger than insects, but as they came closer it was possible to make out their diaphanous white robes, blowing in the breeze as they danced. One figure seemed to be playing a pipe.

'Let's go and talk to them,' said Marsyas. 'They'll know where to find Hades's palace.'

Dionysos's eyes opened wide; but Marsyas had already started to scramble across the meadow. The god, terrified he might be left behind, followed after him.

Crouching low, like the expert tracker that he was, Marsyas ran to the cover of a pile of rocks, from where he could get a good look at the white-clad figures. Dionysos scuttled after him. When they were both hidden, they peeped out. No more than twenty feet away, the little procession was forming into a circle. It seemed that either they had not noticed Marsyas and Dionysos, or else they had noticed and they didn't care. When they had arranged themselves, they stood silently for a second or two, and then, amid a clattering of finger-cymbals, they started to sing. Their ringleader, a tall man with an impressive white beard, tootled meanderingly on the flute.

'What are they doing?' asked Dionysos.

'Shhh!' said Marsyas. 'Listen!'

O, Iakkhos! O, Iakkhos!
  don't smite us, don't whack us,
we're pious, we're wholly sincere;

We implore you, O, Iakkhos:
  Please help us! Please back us!
Please answer our prayers and draw near!

'Who's Iakkhos?' asked Marsyas. Then he looked at Dionysos, and saw that the god was sweating in terror.

'*I* am Iakkhos,' Dionysos god said. 'It is one of my epithets.'

'That's all right then. Let's give them a shout.'

'No!' Dionysos reached out a trembling hand to stop Marsyas. 'They might be dangerous!'

But it was too late. The satyr had already hopped over the rocks. 'Halloo!' he called. 'Halloo!'

The pious devotees fell silent. Their leader's beard twitched with cold fury. He held up a hand to still the rest of the disciples, and he turned his deep-set eyes to Marsyas. 'Stranger,' he said, 'how dare you interrupt our ceremony?'

'I've brought Iakkhos to see you!' Marsyas said. 'He's there, hiding behind those rocks.'

The devotee scowled. 'Iakkhos does not hide,' he said.

'But he does. Take a look!' Marsyas pointed to the rocks. 'Go on,' he said.

The devotee sighed. 'Come out!' he called.

Dionysos popped his head over the rock. Then, almost apologetically, the god straightened up.

'Come,' the devotee said.

Meekly, Dionysos did as he was asked. The god stood before the holy man, who was at least a foot taller. The holy man examined Dionysos carefully. He looked into his dark eyes. He reached out to feel the beard upon the god's face. He felt the muscles of his arms. Then he stepped back and whispered a few words to one of the white-clad acolytes, a woman with lank hair and a sallow face.

'We do not recognise you,' he said, turning back to face Dionysos.

Marsyas snickered. 'What do you mean you do not recognise me?' Dionysos asked.

'Iakkhos is noble and proud. He stands tall, with fire in his eyes. But you, my friend, are as timid as an abducted virgin.'

Despite his fear, Dionysos's pride was pricked. 'But I *am* Iakkhos!' he said. He meant it to sound commanding, but instead it sounded petulant.

The devotee smiled a disdainful smile. 'Go on your way, stranger. Leave us to our devotions.'

Dionysos could not let the challenge pass. He swallowed hard, then he said, 'My name is Dionysos, who is also called

Iakkhos. It is I who brought the gift of wine to the people of the world and I *demand* that you honour me.'

The holy man sighed. 'Go on your way,' he said again. 'Do not commit these blasphemies again.'

'But it *is* me! Do you not recognise me?' the exasperated Dionysos protested.

The holy man had heard enough. He threw his flute to one side and lunged towards the god. He grabbed Dionysos by the beard and wrestled him to the ground. Dionysos fell on his back. Then the holy man was on top of him, pinning him down. A terrible stench of piety filled Dionysos's nostrils. The god tried to struggle against his assailant, but he felt strangely weak. The holy man set about giving Dionysos a beating. The other acolytes gathered round and chanted hymns.

Fake Iakkhos! Sham godling!
Let's smite him, let's whack him,
for taking our god's name in vain.

This ersatz redeemer,
impostor, blasphemer—
let's smite him! Let's whack him again!

Marsyas, fearing that Dionysos would be beaten to a pulp, noticed the abandoned flute on the ground. He grabbed it and put it to his lips. Then, with one long breath, he played a phrase of such great and astonishing melancholy that the mob suddenly became still. Tears filled the holy man's eyes. He stopped his pummelling.

Marsyas played the phrase again.

The bearded man collapsed on top of Dionysos, overcome

with emotion. The other acolytes sank to the ground where they burst into tears.

Marsyas took the flute from his lips. 'Pssst!' he said to the god. 'Dionysos! Let's scarper.'

The god wriggled free from the sobbing man. Marsyas brandished the flute. 'And I'm going to keep hold of this. You never know when it might be useful.'

Then Marsyas and Dionysos left the devotees to their sobbing and hurtled across the meadow and towards the grey cliffs that loomed in the distance. When they could no longer see the devotees—the acolytes or Iakkholytes or what-have-you—they slowed to a walk.

'We must be getting there,' Marsyas said. 'It can't be far.'

Dionysos trailed behind the satyr, feeling less of a god than he had felt for a very long time.

37

At last they reached the distant cliffs that rose sheer up from the plains. Great walls of grey, they were entirely unscaleable, even to a goatling like Marsyas. 'Left or right?' Dionysos asked.

Marsyas looked up at the cliff. 'I have no idea,' he said.

'Are you not supposed to be my guide?' Dionysos asked him.

'Now, don't get sulky, Dionysos. We've got all the time in the underworld. How about we go left first? If we don't find anything interesting, we can turn round.'

The god sighed. 'Lead the way,' he said.

They followed the foot of the cliff, and as they walked, Marsyas realised that he had been neither hungry nor thirsty since their descent into Hades. He didn't really want anything. He didn't even *want* to want anything.

Eventually they came to a steep path cut into the cliff. They started to climb. The path zigzagged back and forth until it came to a narrow passage that cut directly into the cliff face. They squeezed into the passage and walked through the darkness, emerging on a wooded plateau where clusters of willows stood forlorn against the sky. Ahead of them was a path, fringed by poplars—black on the left and white on the right—and the path wound its way to the doors of a dark, looming palace. The palace seemed to exude an atmosphere of despair.

Dionysos stopped. 'This must be the place,' Marsyas said.

They moved on. There was no breeze. The sky hung low over their heads. The poplars rustled as they passed, as if they were trying to communicate some great sadness. The closer they came to the palace, the more Dionysos was filled by a strange, indeterminate sense of dread. He tiptoed down the avenue behind Marsyas. The great palace rose up in front of them, unwelcoming. They came to the tall door, cast from a dark, cold metal.

'Shall I knock?' Marsyas asked.

'Knock? Should we not just wait a little while?' Dionysos's face was pale.

'For what?' asked Marsyas. Then he hammered on the door. 'Oi! Oi! Oi!' he yelled. 'You in there! Come out!'

'Do you not think that you should be a bit more polite?' asked Dionysos.

Marsyas pounded again on the door. 'Oi, you gloomy lot! Let us in!'

The poplars and willows whispered and sighed, as if in reply.

Marsyas was becoming impatient now. 'Open the door you halfwit moles,' he hollered. 'Come out or there'll be trouble.'

From inside came the sound of shuddering and creaking. Then a servant opened the door. He was tall and thickly built, and his face was like a diseased gourd. 'And who are you?' the servant asked.

'I'm Marsyas the satyr. And this is the god Dionysos.'

Dionysos nodded. To his relief, this time he was not challenged. 'A living mortal and an immortal travelling together in the land of the dead?' the servant said. 'How strange! Who have you come to see?'

'Who do you think?' Marsyas said.

'I am not playing guessing games, goat boy. I asked you a question.'

'Tell me who's asking,' Marsyas said. 'I don't want to waste my breath on some low-ranking official.'

The servant sighed. 'I am Hades's servant, holder of the keys.' He rattled a clutch of wooden keys that hung by his side.

'Nice job,' said Marsyas.

'It's not bad,' the servant shrugged. 'We don't get many visitors. It's pretty quiet, to tell the truth. And that suits me just fine.'

'So,' Marsyas said, 'can we come in?'

The servant leaned over and sniffed at Marsyas and Dionysos. His nose crinkled, then he straightened up again. 'No,' he said. 'I'd rather you didn't.' Then he pushed the door shut. Marsyas and Dionysos heard the sound of a key turning in the lock.

Dionysos glared at Marsyas. 'A lot of good you are,' he grumbled. 'Here, let me.' He tapped on the door. 'Hello! Hades!' he called, his voice reedy and timid. 'It is your cousin, Dionysos. Let me in.'

There was a long pause.

'Hello! It is I, Dionysos!'

Silence.

'You and your cousin were close, were you?' asked Marsyas, curling his lip into a sneer.

Dionysos sat down with his back against the door. He looked back at the sighing willows and the poplars, and all at once he was overcome with a sense of terrible futility.

‘What has become of me?’ Dionysos sighed. ‘Up there I was loved and feared. Here everyone just ignores me. Except my disciples. And they just attack me.’

Marsyas sat down by Dionysos’s side and—out of boredom more than anything else—put the purloined flute to his lips. He blew gently. A soft, sweet melody, no more than a snippet, hung on the air and was gone. He blew again, an answering phrase. Then a third, and a fourth. The music seemed muffled and distant, but it was calming in a way. He could hear Dionysos sobbing beside him. The satyr went on playing.

Then, to his surprise, there was a rattling of keys and a creaking of hinges, and the doors of the palace opened again. But this time it was not the gourd-faced servant. Instead, it was a young maid. She was lovely, pale and sad. Once—before the rabbit-skins—Marsyas might have desired her. But now he just felt a kind of kinship, as if he was joined to her in sorrow. ‘Hello,’ he said, taking the flute from his lips.

‘Was that your music?’ she asked, her lip trembling.

‘It was.’

‘Oh! I’ve been down here so long. I’ve not heard music for what seems like an eternity. I’m serving-maid to Hades and Persephone, and they don’t permit music in their court.’ She hesitated and squinted at Marsyas. ‘Who are you, and what are you doing here?’

‘I’m Marsyas,’ said the satyr. ‘The snivelling one over there is my friend Dionysos.’

‘You play beautifully,’ the girl said.

‘You think so?’

‘Oh yes. Could you play something else?’

‘If you like,’ the satyr said. He put the flute to his lips and played another tune.

When he came to the end, the maid was looking at him with a terrible sadness. 'How beautiful!' she said. 'How very beautiful! I don't know how long it has been . . .'

'So, can we come in?' asked Marsyas.

The girl smiled. 'Of course,' she said.

The satyr and the god followed the serving maid into the gloomy palace. The black marble was oppressive. Darkness gathered in the corners and up in the high-vaulted ceiling. The serving maid went ahead. Dionysos and Marsyas followed her down the hallway, and up the stairs at the far end.

They emerged into the throne room.

Seated side-by-side on their black thrones, with long, pale faces, were Hades and his poor, pale, pomegranate-stained wife, Persephone.

38

The two gods of the underworld gazed at the new arrivals, but they did not register a flicker of interest. Marsyas thought he heard Persephone sigh.

'Hades!' Dionysos said. He felt more at ease now that he was in the company of gods, his own kind, 'It is I, Dionysos!'

Hades paused, then his mouth moved. His voice was soft to the point of being inaudible.

'Speak up a bit,' said Marsyas. 'You're mumbling.'

Hades repeated himself, a little louder. 'I said that I see who you are. But tell me, Dionysos: who is the one who stinks of goat? Why did you bring him here?'

'He is my servant,' Dionysos said.

'Servant?' Marsyas protested. Dionysos shushed him.

'Your servant? And tell me, Dionysos, is he *alive*? I mean, is he *not dead*?'

'Yes,' said Dionysos quietly. 'I mean, no. He is not dead.'

'You should not have brought him,' said Hades. 'It causes a terrible mess when you have the living poking around in Hades. Anyway, Dionysos, what brings you and your servant here to the underworld?'

'I have come for my mother, Semele,' Dionysos said. 'I have come to deliver her from this gloomy kingdom.'

'Your mother?' Hades opened his eyes rather wide, and then, as if choosing his words very carefully indeed, said, 'Dionysos—have you ever *met* your mother?'

Dionysos hesitated. 'No,' he said. 'Why?'

Hades turned to his wife. 'Persephone, dear, could you run and fetch Semele?'

The pale goddess nodded her head. She climbed down from the throne with funereal grace and swept out of the room. Hades smiled to himself.

'Why do you smile, Hades?' asked Dionysos.

'I am sentimental, Dionysos. The thought of your reunion with your mother gladdens my heart. Ah—here she comes!'

They heard a voice, high pitched and shrill. 'If it's that no-good son of mine,' the voice trilled, 'tell him that I am furious. Leaving me down here for aeons—is that a way to treat a mother? Dionysos? Is that you? How could you! Your poor mother . . .'

Into the throne room burst a woman impressive in her magnitude. She had blackened hair, as if burned by a fire, and a pale sour face. Poor Semele: since Zeus had displayed himself in all his glory and burned her to a crisp, she had found herself cooped up in the underworld with no company save Hades himself, the dreary Persephone and the servants, and she had nothing to do but to wander around and converse with twittering shades under the sighing willows and poplars.

'Where is he?' she demanded. 'Which one is my son?'

'Mother,' said Dionysos. 'I have come to fetch you and to bring you to Olympos.'

'You?' she shrieked. 'You are Dionysos? Look at you!

You are thin as a plank! You need feeding. And who is the goat?'

Marsyas took a bow. 'Marsyas, Ma'am,' he said. 'A satyr of Phrygia.'

Semele turned away from the satyr. 'Oh, Dionysos, you would not believe how terrible it has been down here. They are all so gloomy and ponderous. Day after day after day with their long faces. Really you are quite, quite cruel to leave your mother here for so long.'

She went on like this for a long time. Every time it seemed that she had run out of things to say, Dionysos opened his mouth to speak. But before he could do so, Semele drew breath and continued. Marsyas picked the dirt of the underworld out of his fingernails and waited for her to finish.

When she was done, there was silence. Dionysos turned to Hades. 'Well,' he said, 'if you have no objection, then we ask your permission to leave.'

'Of course,' said the god of the underworld. He gave a genial wave of the hand. 'But how we will miss you, Semele.' His smile was thin and insincere.

'Can we go, then?' Marsyas asked.

'Not only *can* you go,' said Hades, 'but you *must*.'

They stood there in silence for a short while. 'Just one thing, Hades,' Dionysos said, 'how do we . . .'

'Find your way out?' asked Hades. He laughed a dry and scratchy laugh. 'You will not get Kharon to take you back over the river, that's for sure. He's a stickler, is Kharon. So you will have to take another path. It is the path that the unfortunate Orpheus took. It is also the way that Persephone, my lovely bride, ascends every spring. But you must be careful: once you are on the path, you must neither look back nor sit down until you are back in the sunlight. If you do either, then you will have to stay here forever.'

'That all seems a bit arbitrary,' said Marsyas.

The god shrugged. 'This is how it has always been,' he said. 'Now, Persephone, please show our guests the way.'

'Of course,' she said. Persephone rose from her throne and gestured to the little party. She was demure, compliant and absolutely impossible to read. 'Follow me,' she said.

With Persephone gliding ahead, the company of travellers made their way out of the palace by the rear entrance. Next in line behind Persephone was Dionysos. Then came Marsyas. Last of all was Semele, haranguing her son from the rear for his negligence and lack of filial care.

They headed up a small slope, and through a cleft in the rock that led to a steep upward path. They walked for a long while. As they climbed, the itching beneath Marsyas's skin returned. It was almost—almost, but not quite—a relief to be able to *feel* something after the muffled stagnation of the lower reaches of Hades; but along with the itch came the terrible ache of desire. The satyr thought of his skin hanging in Apollo's quarters up on Olympos, and of the agonising memory of his suffering as Hermes had peeled him like a ripe fruit. He began to scratch and twitch. He bleated and dropped a few anxious turds. Dionysos's mother carefully stepped around them.

I want my skin back, Marsyas thought. *I want my skin back!*

The party emerged into a chamber dripping with water. Overhead, bats burbled high-pitched monologues.

'This is it,' Persephone said, and she pointed to a place further ahead where, high up and accessible only by a precariously slippery staircase, a shaft of light was coming through a crevice.

'Are you saying that we are to go up there and through that hole?' Marsyas asked.

'It is the only way.'

They thanked Persephone and wished her farewell, then they started up the stairs that led out of the underworld. Persephone watched them climb.

Marsyas went ahead. Semele followed behind, with Dionysos bringing up the rear. It was an exhausting climb, and it was hard not to give in to the temptation to sit down or glance back over their shoulders. But soon Marsyas could smell, not far above, the fragrance of pinewoods, the cold, brisk chill of winter driving away the stultifying deadness of Hades. He quickened his pace. He could hear Semele behind him, muttering reprimands to her son.

Marsyas reached the fissure in the earth and squeezed through. The shock of the sunlight on his fur made him shudder. Then he called back, 'I'm through! Who's next?'

He heard Semele's voice, small and frightened, coming from the earth. 'It is too small. I will not fit.'

Marsyas did not give her the chance to argue. He reached into the earth and grabbed her head, Dionysos shoved her from behind. Semele bellowed in protest. For a moment she was stuck. Far below, Persephone saw the light blotted out. She could hear, over the sound of twitter bats, Semele's curses and Dionysos's grunts as he tried to push his mother through the hole.

Semele's head emerged, like a new-born baby, then her shoulders, next her arms. 'Oooh!' she moaned. 'It is too tight! Stop!'

Dionysos gave her a final push. 'Dionysos! Stop!' she yelled. But then it was all over. There was a dull plop, and out she came.

Marsyas let go and tumbled backwards down the bank. Semele flopped down on the grass and moaned. Dionysos crept out into the light, a little ashamed at having subjected his mother to such indignities.

Far below, Persephone, the Lady of the Underworld, looked up at the light. Soon, she would begin her annual journey up into the light as well. But it was not yet time. She turned her back on the light and, slow and solitary, she returned to the palace.

39

Marsyas, Dionysos and Semele sat on the rocks, recovering their strength. It was still the tail end of winter. The weather was cold, the sun low in the sky and birds singing in the trees. But it was one of those beautiful days on which it is possible to detect the first traces of spring on the air.

'Where are we?' Marsyas asked. He was glad to be back in the sunlight, even if the itching was giving him trouble again.

Dionysos shrugged. 'I do not know. But rather up here than down there.'

'Count yourself lucky,' Semele snapped. 'I have been down there for years.' She turned to Marsyas. 'I am covered in corpse-dust. You there—you little goat or whatever you are—where can I go to get cleaned up?'

Marsyas sniffed the air. 'There's a stream not far off.' He pointed to a path through the rocks.

'A stream? You expect a lady to wash in public like a common prostitute? I want somewhere with four walls, where I can bathe undisturbed.'

'You had better do as she says,' Dionysos whispered to the satyr.

So Marsyas trotted off over the hill. He was trying not to think about the itching, because the more you pay attention to an itch, the worse it becomes. He was trying not to think about Olympos, or about his skin, or about the god Apollo. He was trying not to let hope get the better of him. As he ran, he hummed to himself, to keep these clamouring hopes and fears and itches at bay.

It was not long before he came upon a shepherd, sitting outside his hut and warming himself in the late winter sun with the benign air of the senescent. He was an old man, and he spoke a language that Marsyas did not understand. Marsyas asked in the Phrygian tongue if the shepherd would mind offering his hut for the purposes of bathing a large and ill-tempered woman. The old man smiled and nodded uncomprehendingly. Taking this as an answer in the affirmative, Marsyas ran back to fetch the others.

The old man was a worthy host. He heated hot water over the fire for them to bathe with, and Semele asked the satyr, the shepherd and her son to turn their backs whilst she washed. When she was done, Dionysos and Marsyas splashed water over themselves also, washing themselves clean of the dust of the dead. Whilst the god and the satyr cleaned themselves, the old man, forgetting his age, attempted to tempt Semele with caresses. She slapped him hard on the cheek.

When they had washed the death-dust from their skins and the gloomy light of Hades from their eyes, they feasted on peasant bread, cheese, olives and quantities of wine. How sweet it tasted! Marsyas felt almost happy as he licked the salty residue of the cheese from his fingers.

The sun set and Dionysos turned to Marsyas. 'You remember that corpse?' he said.

'Which one?'

'The one who gave you the barley cakes. Did you not say you would deliver some kind of message? Something about a wife of his who lived in Didyma or somewhere. I am sure that there was something about fish.'

'Fish?' Marsyas shrugged. He really could not remember much. Everything about the underworld seemed to be cloaked in the greyness of forgetting. 'I don't suppose it matters,' the satyr said.

The three of them sat in silence as the sun sank behind the hills. When the sky darkened, the shepherd broke into song. The song was strange and mournful. Marsyas scratched now and then. Dionysos looked up to the sky. 'Soon the path to Olympos will appear,' he said.

'About time too,' said Semele.

The first stars emerged, then the broad road of the Milky Way, stretching across the heavens. 'Come, it is time to leave,' Dionysos said.

Marsyas craned his head to look up at the sky. 'But how do we get up there?' he asked.

'Follow me,' said the god.

They thanked the shepherd, and with Dionysos going ahead, the three of them clambered up to a nearby peak. From there it was possible to step onto the road of the Milky Way. Marsyas was astonished by how easy it was—as easy as leaping from the bank to a boulder in the middle of a stream. He looked down. There was something giddying about seeing all those stars at his feet.

'Better not to look down,' Dionysos said. 'Come, it is quite safe.'

Dionysos went first, his beard pointed and his eyes narrow. He was followed by Semele, with Marsyas bringing up the rear. They climbed slowly and as they climbed the atmosphere thinned. Marsyas puffed with shortness of breath. Meanwhile Semele, who had suffered the foetid air of the underworld for so long that her lungs were quite unused to this bracing climate, seemed to heave bodily with every single breath that she took. Marsyas felt his breath frosting on his little goat's beard. 'Are we there yet?' he bleated.

Dionysos did not answer.

When they came to the Gate of Clouds, the stars winked out around them, first one and then another, and the earth below passed from view. The clouds wet Marsyas's rabbit-fur coat, making him shiver.

'Marsyas! Semele! Keep close, or you will lose the path.'

They walked through the damp, thin air until they were almost soaked through. Then they emerged into blinding sunlight. Marsyas's fur started to steam.

The god stopped. 'Olympos,' he said. 'Celestial home of all the gods'. Then he smiled a smile of such radiance that the shepherd with whom they had spent the day before looked up into the sky, and saw a momentary flash of brilliance amongst the stars.

PART VI
OLYMPOS

40

They passed through the Gate of Clouds to emerge into the bronze colonnade. Marsyas lifted his snout to catch the scents on the air. There was a sweet sickliness that turned his stomach. It made him think of the god Apollo.

'Come,' Dionysos said. He walked ahead of them to the dark bronze doors at the far end.

Marsyas felt a little giddy and sick. The deep, subcutaneous itch was getting worse. He put his fingernails to his skin and scrabbled at the loose rabbit-pelt. The satyr thought of Kybele. He thought of her warm embrace, her soft breasts. He wanted to be near her. He wanted her to speak soothing words in his ear, to groom the fear from his fur.

Dionysos knocked on the doors. There was no response.

The god knocked again, more impatiently. Marsyas put his hand to the door. The bronze was warm, as if it still remembered the heat of the forge.

'Knock again,' Semele said. 'Knock louder.'

Dionysos knocked a third time. The door opened, just a fraction. It was Hermes. Marsyas recognised his voice—soft, melodious, as irritating as a bed of nettles. 'Who knocks?'

Hearing Hermes's voice, Marsyas almost retched in fear. Dionysos struck him a blow on the back of the head to calm him. 'It is I, Dionysos,' the god said.

Hermes opened the door wider, and raised an eyebrow in welcome. 'Ah! The triumphal train has returned from the East,' he snickered. Then he looked hard at Marsyas.

The satyr met his eyes. For a moment the pain of the flaying knife shuddered through him. 'What is this creature you have brought with you?' asked Hermes.

Dionysos spoke sweetly. 'He is my servant. I have brought him all the way from India.'

Hermes looked at Marsyas a moment longer, as if puzzled. 'What is his name?'

Dionysos hesitated a moment, then said, 'That is a good question. I have never even thought to ask. I just call him "boy", or "you".'

'He is a strange beast,' said Hermes. 'He is hairy.'

'Yes,' said Dionysos. 'I suppose he is.' Then he leaned towards Hermes with a conspiratorial air. 'They all are in India,' he said.

'Really?' Hermes opened his eyes wide.

'Yes, really.'

Hermes thought about this for a moment. 'He looks as if he has about him something of a goat, and something of a man, and also something a little bit *rabbity*.'

'Rabbity? Why, yes. He is part rabbit, I am afraid,' Dionysos said cheerfully. 'It is a sad story. I found him in the Ganges basin, poor creature. His mother had got drunk and coupled with a rabbit. When the child was born, she rejected him, on account of his ugliness, so I took him in. Now, Hermes, are you going to let us in or are you not? My mother has come a long way to talk to Zeus.'

Semele, bringing up the rear, cleared her throat. 'You there with the ankle-wings,' she said. 'Get a move on!'

'Well,' Hermes said, glancing from one to the other of the curious little party, 'I suppose you had better all come in.'

The messenger god led them inside.

When they stepped into the broad courtyard, the first thing that Marsyas thought was how disappointing it all was, how small and how cramped. The courtyard was formal and orderly, but rather barren. It was scattered with stones, the stones covered in lichens and mosses; and in the northwest corner a single tree—one of those stubborn trees that clings to even the topmost reaches of the mountains—raised its dark and twisted branches into the clear air. At the far end, to the east, Marsyas could see the steps that led up to Zeus's throne room whilst to his left, scattered up the slopes to the north, were the gods' chambers. On the other side, a small path led away down the hill. In the distance, Marsyas could hear the *clank! bang! thud!* of the lame god Hephaistos at work in his forge. There was a faint trace of soot and burned beeswax on the air. Further along the southern side of the courtyard was the feasting hall.

In all, the peak of Olympos was not much larger than a middling-sized field in Phrygia. And whilst the marble houses were impressive in their way, no mere peasant dwellings, there was something claustrophobic about the way they were wedged haphazardly into the rocks, one here, one there, as if jostling for position.

Dionysos looked round at the cramped peak, then at his mother's face. Semele seemed ill-tempered. 'This is it?' she asked, hands on her hips.

'This is Olympos, Mother,' Dionysos said.

The muscles around Semele's mouth tightened. 'I cannot say I like the look of it,' she said. 'Where is everyone? At least down *there* I had people to talk to.' She strode into the centre of the courtyard. Hermes hovered around her nervously, not quite sure what to do with her, his tiny ankle wings beating so fast that they were no more than a blur.

The fluttering god led them along a path that climbed north through the rocks, away from the courtyard. They came to marble building fronted by smooth bronze pillars. It was set a little apart from the other dwellings. Hermes paused and touched the pillars lightly. 'These will be your quarters. Hephaistos will forge you new pillars with images displaying your deeds,' the messenger god said. 'If you *have* anything to display, that is.'

Dionysos dismissed Hermes's comment with a wave of his hand. 'Tell me, Hermes, is the old man around?'

'He is sorting out some business elsewhere,' Hermes said. 'He will summon you when he returns. I will leave you to settle in. But what about your servant? Will he stay with you, or shall I send him to the servants' quarters?'

'He can stay with me,' said Dionysos, giving Marsyas a friendly pat on the back.

Hermes hovered by the door, the wings on his heels flapping furiously.

'Thank you. That will be all, Hermes,' Dionysos said.

Hermes wanted to ask Dionysos about India. He wanted to hear about his travels, about the lands to the east. He admired Dionysos, in a way; but he also envied him. He envied him his freedom, the way that he could wander where he chose, whilst Hermes had to always go where he was told. The delivery boy of the gods, he acted on behalf of others, never for himself. But what was most intolerable about Dionysos was this: he *knew* things. He knew things that Hermes—who had never voyaged beyond the Tigris, the Euphrates and the Indus, who had never sat naked with the gymnosophists or tasted the soma that brings knowledge—did not know, and that he would never know.

The god fluttered back down the path towards the courtyard, his cheeks burning with the shame of his abrupt dismissal. Dionysos led Semele and the satyr into the airy bedchamber. There were several couches and low tables scattered here and there. Windows looked north towards Makedonia and the barbarian lands beyond, and west to where the mountains fell towards the sea. It was cool and airy. 'Mother, this will be your home,' Dionysos said.

'I have not got my own place?'

'We can talk about this later. This is a temporary measure, mother.'

Semele made a tutting sound and sat down on one of the couches. Dionysos took another and patted the coverlet. Marsyas sat down beside him, swinging his legs. Semele lay down, stretched herself, and fell immediately asleep. She snored softly.

From where he sat, Marsyas could see out of the western window. He gazed across the clouds and the sea. In the far distance he could see the smoking peak of Etna, and beyond that, the great Pillars of Hercules, after which the great ocean stretched on endlessly to who-knows-where.

'Marsyas,' Dionysos said, 'I need to take a rest. Do not stray too far.'

'All right,' the satyr said. He stood up and padded towards the window, gazing over the distant ocean. Dionysos stretched out on his couch and closed his eyes.

Marsyas was itchy and restless. He paced around the room for a while. Then, bored and oppressed by claustrophobia, he headed out of the bedchamber and back down the path to the courtyard, so that he could have a look around.

41

The satyr went from building to building, sniffing around, stroking the bronze pillars outside each of them, glancing over his shoulder to make sure that he wasn't being watched. He could identify the homes of the various gods by the images engraved on the pillars. Fish, octopuses, lobsters and foamy nymphs indicated that this was the Olympian home of Poseidon; peacocks adorned the pillars outside Here's quarters; Artemis's home was decorated with pretty scenes of cypresses and deer, and the image of a man being torn apart by his own hunting dogs.

Then Marsyas came to the north-eastern side of the courtyard, where there was plain, austere building fashioned of white marble, and there he stopped. Something made the flesh beneath his rabbit coat shudder. He looked more closely at the bronze pillars outside and saw, engraved upon them, a scene that was sickeningly familiar, even though he was seeing it from an angle that was strange and new. There was a satyr hanging from a pine tree, bronze skin stripped from bronze flesh. Around the suspended form clustered nymphs and satyroi, bowing their heads in mourning. And all the terror and suffering and pain of Marsyas's torture was transformed into a perfection of angle and measure, an appalling beauty of form.

He reached out and traced the lines of the etched images with a trembling finger; and it was then that Marsyas saw how it would be in future times, how the image of his suffering would be replicated again and again: by Myron and Zeuxis, by Anselmi and de Ribera, by Titian and Manfredi and Kapoor. 'Ah! I know that story!' people would say. 'See how the foolish Marsyas hangs from the tree by his feet, stretched out like an animal at the butcher's shop. See, there is the god with his knife. Look at how cunning the artist has been, how he depicts a little dog licking the liquid that drips from the wounds. Look at the dark figure of the satyr who carries a bucket, assisting in the murder of his brother. See, there is the old seilenos who sits in the posture of a philosopher, his chin on his hand, his eyes filled with sadness.'

Marsyas drew his hand away. It was then that he realised there was somebody at home. From inside the building came the sound of urgent grunting. Marsyas hesitated, puzzled for a moment. This grunting and puffing was so different from the flurry of yelps and bleats that accompanies the joyful union of satyr and nymph that at first he could not make sense of it. But then he heard the cry of the god Apollo in the moment of climax, and the sob of some poor girl who was pinned underneath him, and Marsyas felt a pang of pity.

There was silence. Marsyas heard footsteps coming towards the door. He padded round the corner of the building and hid himself. When he peeped out, he saw Apollo shove a young girl out into the courtyard. The girl was sobbing. Two servants scurried across the courtyard and took her by the arms. They dragged her back through the courtyard towards the Gate of Clouds. As they dragged her, she looked back over her shoulder and spotted Marsyas in his hiding place. Their eyes met. There was nothing the satyr could do. He ducked back behind the pillars, listening to the sound of her sobbing fade.

Then Apollo appeared again in the doorway. He left the door wide open and crossed the courtyard in the direction of the throne room to the east. The god disappeared into the dark of the building.

Marsyas waited a short while. Seeing that the god had not reappeared, he crept towards the door of Apollo's chambers and peered in. There was a low couch, and a window beside which hung the lyre with its two curved horns and its strings of cow gut. But what took Marsyas's attention was the thing that was hanging on the other side of the window. It was a kind of coat, sleek and soft and furred. The coat glowed with an exquisite red tinge.

It was the pelt of a satyr.

42

Marsyas tiptoed into Apollo's chambers. As he did so, he was startled by a movement out of the corner of his eye. He stopped and looked round. On the wall there was a mirror of burnished bronze. In the mirror he saw a shabby and pitiful creature that he only half recognised. Marsyas trotted over and studied himself. He looked at the slack skin, the face worn down by pain, the trembling hands, the dangling pouch between his legs, the dull, lifeless rabbit fur.

How ugly I've become, he thought.

The satyr padded over to Apollo's couch. He could see the damp stain of the god's lust still drying on the sheets. He poked the stain with his finger and licked his fingertip thoughtfully. It tasted of salt and bitterness.

Next he examined the lyre. He reached out his hand to the strings, not quite touching them. Then he drew back, because he was afraid. He wanted to take the lyre and hurl it from the window, to let it smash on the rocks below; but he could not bring himself to touch it. He turned his attention to the pelt. He reached out to stroke the soft fur. His flesh tingled and tugged, as if it longed to be reunited.

'Boy!'

The satyr drew back his hand. Apollo was standing in the doorway.

'What are you doing, boy?'

Marsyas pulled his hand away from the pelt as if scalded. 'Nothing,' he said.

The god stepped towards him. 'Nothing?' Apollo laughed. 'Tell me who you are. We have not been introduced.'

Can it be that he doesn't recognise me? thought Marsyas.

'I'm Dionysos's boy,' the satyr said.

Apollo smiled. 'Ah, the exotic Indian creature.'

Marsyas smiled ingratiatingly. 'Yes, Sir.'

Apollo smiled back. 'Well, boy,' the god said, 'I am tired. It has been a long day and I need is to relax. Can you help me?'

'Me?'

'Yes, you. Come, take this pot of oil. Give me a rub.' Apollo indicated towards a jar in the corner.

'A rub?' Marsyas nodded. 'Yes,' he said, 'Yes, of course.'

The satyr opened the jar and sniffed. It was olive oil. Apollo sat down on the couch and beckoned to him. Marsyas carried the jar over and dipped his hands into the greenish liquid. 'Go on, boy,' said Apollo.

Marsyas started to rub the oil into the god's skin.

'Make me shine!' Apollo said. 'Make me shine like a bronze pot!'

As Marsyas rubbed, his flesh itched appallingly, but he did not dare scratch.

Apollo grunted. 'You Indian boys know how to use your hands. Go on, move them a little lower.'

Marsyas moved his hands down to Apollo's belly.

The god adjusted his robe. 'No, lower still.'

Falteringly, Marsyas opened up Apollo's robes and wrapped his hands around Apollo's cock. The god sighed. 'Slowly, now,' he said.

Marsyas tugged and pulled until Apollo spurted his seed for a second time that day. It was thick, milky, and ice-cold. Apollo's bronzed body shuddered. The god lay back on his couch with his eyes closed and he reached out a hand to stroke Marsyas by the ears. 'Boy,' he said, 'You may look funny, but Dionysos knows what he is doing in having you as a servant. Now, wipe your hands and bring me my lyre.'

Marsyas wiped his hands on the coverlet. He went over to where the lyre was hanging on the wall. When he picked it up, the faint thrum of the strings made him feel queasy. He handed the lyre to Apollo. The god closed his eyes.

The satyr scuttled out of the Apollo's quarters, back across the courtyard, and up the track that led to Dionysos's bedchamber.

43

When he got back, he found the god still lying on the bed with closed eyes. Semele had gone. Hearing Marsyas come in, the god sat up. 'How are you doing, little fellow?' he asked.

Marsyas did not reply. He sat down on the couch and disconsolately tugged at his rabbit-skin coat.

'It will not be long,' Dionysos said. 'Just be patient, and you will have your skin back.'

Then a gong sounded across the peak of Olympos, and Dionysos smiled. 'That is a summons to the feasting hall,' he said. 'Nectar and ambrosia. Strictly for immortals only. I will fetch you something back to eat. There is usually some mortal food around.' The god Dionysos hesitated. 'Marsyas,' he said, 'you look gloomy. Where have you been?'

'Just looking round,' the satyr mumbled.

'Oh,' said the god. 'You have not seen my mother on your travels, have you?'

Marsyas shook his head. But at that moment there was a shout. 'Dionysos! Are you up at last? What is happening now?'

Semele came in. From the look on her face, Dionysos assumed that her first impressions of Olympos had not been favourable. 'Mother,' the god said, 'let us go and eat. The gods are waiting.'

Marsyas watched as the two of them left for the feasting hall. When they were gone, he trotted back down to the courtyard just in time to see Apollo also leaving his chambers and heading in the same direction. The god glowed softly with a sheen of olive oil and pride, and he had his lyre tucked under his arm. He did not glance at the satyr as he passed. Marsyas was sure now that nobody up here, not even Apollo, recognised him. And why should they? It was not just his rabbit-skin coat that made him anonymous. It was also his *unimportance*.

Marsyas sat on a moss-covered rock and waited a while longer. He could hear the *clang! clang! clang!* of Hephaistos's forge. Not longer after, Athene appeared from her chambers, in full battle dress. She whisked across the courtyard, passing by the satyr as if he didn't exist, and strode into the feasting hall. Next, Zeus emerged from the throne room, looking preoccupied, and went to join the feast. Hermes whirred past, followed by Aphrodite, Demeter, Artemis, Here and Ares. There was no sign of Poseidon, who preferred to spend his time down in the oceans back on earth.

From the feasting hall came strains of sweet burbling song, and the sound of raised voices as the Olympians bragged, argued and flirted. A little while later, the clanging from the forge stopped. Hephaistos appeared at the top of the steps on the southern side of the courtyard, limping slowly. He was sooty and grizzled. He hobbled into the darkness of the hall, and then the courtyard was peaceful. Marsyas caught the sound of plucked harmonies on the lyre. Apollo was playing to accompany the feast.

Now is the time, Marsyas thought. He tiptoed across the courtyard to Apollo's chambers and stepped inside. He did not glance at the bronzed mirror on the wall. Instead he trotted over to where the pelt was hanging by the window and put his hand to it. It gave him a perverse pleasure to stroke the skin that had been stripped from his own body. He rubbed his cheek against the fur.

Marsyas unhooked the skin and lifted it down. The drunken shouts of the gods in the feasting hall sounded like a distant storm. In the heart of the storm, Marsyas could still make out the beautiful, terrible sounds of Apollo's lyre.

The satyr placed the skin down on the couch. Then, trying not to glance at himself in the mirror he started to untie the bows that held the rabbit-skin covering fast. He undid the bows all the way down to his groin. He thought that the skin would come away easily, but it seemed to have become stuck to his flesh. It pulled away only with difficulty.

The satyr bleated in pain as he pulled at the skin.

Maaaeee-he-he . . .
maaaeee-he-he . . .
maaaeee-he-he . . .

He tore the skin away from his chest. It was agonising to strip himself bare like this; but it was too late to go back. Just as it is impossible to avoid picking at a scab that has come half loose, Marsyas now wanted rid of the skin. He tugged again. The skin came away from his belly. He yanked another time, then paused to catch his breath, shaking and panting.

Next, Marsyas peeled back the skin from his shoulders.

Then he jerked it hard and struggled until his right arm was free. He freed his left arm in the same way. As he did so, he caught sight of himself reflected in the mirror, peeled raw and sticky as tar.

He stood on one leg and tugged at the other. Ripples of fiery pain ran down from his hip to his ankle, but the skin came free. He changed legs, standing on the leg that was now naked, and pulled at the other.

Then Marsyas was unclothed. He held the rabbit-skin coat in his hand and let it fall. His body throbbed and pulsed with pain. He reached down to pick up his pelt from the couch. He carefully unfurled it. Working quickly, Marsyas wrapped the skin around his shins and his calves, made sure that it fitted snugly by the knees. After this, he started to work on his thighs, his cock, his belly. He wrapped the skin round one arm, and then the other.

He stopped to rest, the skin still hanging open at his chest. It was only then that he realised the sound of Apollo's lyre had ceased.

Marsyas tipped his head to one side and listened hard. He could hear the shouts of the Olympians, the ebb and flow of their squabbles; but there was no lyre.

The satyr turned to the door. Apollo was standing outside, the lyre in his hand.

'Oh,' the god said. 'So it is *you*.'

44

Apollo stepped inside the bedchamber and kicked the rabbit-skin coat to one side. He placed his lyre down.

Marsyas backed away.

'Marsyas, is it not? The Phrygian satyr?' Apollo said. 'And I thought that you were dead. Well, you are a brave little goat to make it all the way up here.' He reached out as if to stroke Marsyas's cheek.

The satyr took another step backwards. He started to gather the skin that was still hanging lose around his chest and belly; like a cold man in a storm, he fumbled to close up the great, raw gash in front of him. But his fingers were trembling with fear. They were not deft enough. The skin slipped against his flesh.

'You are a brave goat,' Apollo said, 'but you are a foolish one. Come on. Give it back. Give me back my skin.'

Marsyas's lips trembled. 'No,' he bleated.

Then Apollo lurched towards him. With caprine nimbleness, Marsyas leapt onto the couch, scrabbling furiously to close up the wound that ran down his chest and belly. Apollo grabbed at him again, but Marsyas darted sideways, out of the door.

The satyr scampered across the courtyard. The god Apollo turned and gave chase.

Marsyas looked round, wondering where to run to. To the east was Zeus's throne room. To the south was the feasting hall. The doors at to the west that led to the Gate of Clouds were closed. Then he saw the steps that led down to Hephaistos's forge. He made for the steps, scuttling down them quicker than the god could give chase, and he plunged into the darkness of the forge.

Inside, the air was thick with the acrid smell of smoke and burned beeswax. The smelting fire blazed in the centre of the forge, red and gold, turning to white at its very heart. An invisible flue sucked the smoke upwards. The fire hissed and roared and spat. There was a jumbled pile of old broken moulds, fashioned from clay and stone, in one corner. It was dark and shadowy. Marsyas ducked behind them. He looked round. A shaft of sunlight came from the only window, in the southern wall. Marsyas felt his heart pounding. With each beat, ribbons of pain spread out from his chest. He saw the god enter the forge, sniffing the air; but the smell of the forge was too strong, and Apollo could not catch Marsyas's scent, nor could he see him in the darkness.

'I know you are in there, satyr,' the god yelled above the din.

Marsyas pressed his open skin together, trying to get it to join again with his flesh, but the black dust of the forge was already coating his raw flesh, and the skin wouldn't stick. *I need to wash it clean*, Marsyas thought. *I need clean water*. He looked around, but there was only metal and wood and stone and fire.

Apollo took another step forwards. He picked up a half-fashioned sword that was lying to one side, and swung it hard, bringing it down upon an anvil. The sword clanged. 'Come out!' he roared. 'There is nowhere to run to.'

Marsyas watched Apollo from the shadows. The god was blocking the door. His only chance was the window. He crept towards it, keeping out of the shaft of light. Sword in hand, Apollo started to prod and poke at the darkness, describing broad sweeping movements, seeking out the satyr. Marsyas, skilled tracker that he was, moved silently from his hiding place as Apollo stepped further into the room. The god knew that Marsyas could not possibly escape. Olympos was small, and hiding places were few. He clanged the sword on anvils and broken statues, with each blow, letting up a cry.

Clang! 'Come out you fucker!'

Crash! 'I can see you, you piece of goat-shit!'

Clank! 'You cannot escape, you know.'

Marsyas was close to the window now, but not close enough. Apollo was closing in on him. The god's gaze swept to and fro, as he swung the sword, *clank! clank! clank!*

I need to distract him, Marsyas thought.

The satyr reached down and fumbled on the floor in the darkness. His fingers found a hunk of raw, unsmelted copper ore. He picked it up. The ore was heavy, but it fitted perfectly into his palm. It was warm to the touch. Across the forge, in the light of the smelting fire, Marsyas could see a pile of broken sculptures, waiting to be melted down and fashioned into something new. There were arms, legs, torsos, heads, parts of sea monsters. Very slowly, so as not to attract Apollo's attention, Marsyas drew back his arm. Then he waited until Apollo was looking the other way, and threw the lump of ore in a low arc. It cleared the pile of sculptures and clattered behind them. Apollo turned round and let out a snarl of pleasure. 'So that's where you are,' he said, addressing himself to the pile of severed bronze body parts.

Marsyas took his chance. He crouched down a little more, then he hopped onto the windowsill. He was going to take a second leap when he looked down and hesitated, motionless on the sill. Below him was a sheer drop, a black granite cliff-face that plunged for several fathoms until it was lost in the clouds. There was not a single foothold. Had it been a cliff like any other, he could have leapt out and scampered down the craggy slopes with such goatish speed that not even the god Apollo could have kept pace. But this wall of granite was so terrifyingly steep that, even for a goat, it was giddying.

The hesitation was his undoing. Apollo spun round, saw the satyr haloed in the light of the window, and lunged at him. He caught hold of the flap of skin hanging loose at the satyr's chest, and he tugged at it with all his strength.

There was a terrible tearing.

The skin came clean away. Apollo fell back a step and steadied himself. Marsyas, torn again from the scabbard of his skin, stood on the windowsill, red and naked in the evening light. He bleated in agony.

Maaaeee-he-he . . .

Apollo held up the skin for him to see. 'This is mine!' he shouted at the satyr. 'This skin is mine, to do with as I choose. Are you so very fucking ignorant that you do not understand that?'

Marsyas bleated again.

Maaaeee . . .

The god held the skin over the smelting fire. 'This will not happen again,' he said. 'This time, your skin is gone for good.'

Then the god let the pelt fall. There was a brief flowering of sparks. Apollo poked the skin with the half-forged sword, watching it flare, listening to its crackle and sizzle. The skin, in a moment, became soot and ash.

Apollo let the sword drop. It clattered to the floor. He was empty-handed.

Shivering and naked, Marsyas stood on the windowsill, the great void behind him, the evening breezes prickling his back with pain.

Apollo advanced towards him. 'Come here,' he said softly. 'Come!'

Then Marsyas turned his back to the god and faced the great emptiness.

His hands held fast to the sides of the window.

His toes curled and gripped at the sill.

He looked down at the clouds beneath.

His muscles clenched.

Then Marsyas sprang. Away from the sill, away from the forge and the bronze and marble of Olympos, far out into the void.

He bleated as he fell.

Maaaeee-he-he . . .
maaaeee-he-he . . .
maaaeee-he-he . . .

Apollo came to the window and leaned out in time to see the satyr's raw and bloodied form plummeting downwards, until it was swallowed by cloud.

Maaaeee-he-he . . .
maaaeee-he-he . . .
maaaeee-he-he . . .

45

Apollo turned away from the window. He walked back out of the forge. Outside, he crouched down by a small spring that bubbled from the earth. His hands were sticky with blood and soot. The god squatted down and washed his hands clean. Then he straightened up and climbed back up the steps.

In the courtyard he sat down on a rock for a moment to try and clear his thoughts. He could hear the sound of the feast going on, the usual clamour of argument and boasting. He had no more appetite for feasting and celebration today. His head was thumping. He wanted solitude. He wanted peace. He wanted the consolations of his lyre.

The god returned to his chambers. He lay down upon his couch and closed his eyes.

It was then that he heard it—a sound, coming as if from far off. It was something like the bleating of a goat, and something like the buzzing of bees.

Maaaeee-he-he . . .

The god sat up. He shook his head to dislodge the irritating buzzing. But the sound remained stubbornly, unarguably *there.*

Maaaeee-he-he . . .

Apollo pressed his hands to his ears. The sound became louder, not quieter.

Maaaeee-he-he . . .
maaaeee-he-he . . .
maaaeee-he-he . . .

That fucking goat, he thought.

Apollo reached for his lyre and started to pluck at the strings. The music was sweet and delicate, exquisite in its perfection. It drove all cares and worries from his heart, all buzzing and bleating from his ears. It cleansed him. He felt his spirit begin to settle.

The god Apollo played until his heart was calm once more. Then he put down the lyre and closed his eyes.

There it was again. Incessant, continuous, throbbing like a hive.

Maaaeee-he-he . . .
maaaeee-he-he . . .
maaaeee-he-he . . .

The god stood up and went to look out of the window. He could see the sun setting to the west. It was a beautiful evening. The world was clear and perfect and pure. But the sound still continued.

Maaaeee-he-he . . .
maaaeee-he-he . . .
maaaeee-he-he . . .

Apollo spat out of the window. He clutched at his ears. He beat his fists against the side of his head. He squeezed his eyes shut. His whole body was filled with a useless, restless fury.

Why must they ruin everything? he thought.

Why do they always ruin everything?

ACKNOWLEDGEMENTS

This book has had a long and particularly strange evolution. Along the way, many friends, acquaintances and fellow writers have offered me encouragement. This time round, thanks should go, in particular, to the following people: to Dr. Sabira Ståhlberg, Kathy Bell and Jonathan Taylor, whose encouragement and insightful comments on drafts of the manuscript have been invaluable; to my fellow reinventor of Greek myths, the poet Simon Perril; to the musician Sam Williams, who was there at the very beginning; to my agent Marilyn Malin, who has been in it for the long haul; to Suman Chakraborty at Roman Books for his enthusiasm; and finally, as ever, to Elee Kirk for her wise counsel and endless patient reading of manuscripts.

The epigraph with which this book begins comes from H.E. Bates's 1909 translation of Apuleius, 'The Apologia and Florida of Apuleius of Madaura'.

ABOUT THE AUTHOR

Will Buckingham is a novelist and philosopher. He is currently Reader in Writing and Creativity at De Montfort University. His novel *The Descent of the* Lyre, also published by ROMAN Books, was shortlisted for the East Midlands Book Award 2012. *Goat Music* is his fourth novel.